Wanted by a Texas Ranger

KATHRYN KALEIGH

HISTORICAL WESTERN ROMANCES

(Reading Order)

Wanted by a Texas Ranger

Accidentally Alluring

Accidentally Married

Finding Natalie

Promising Samantha

Falling for Allyson

Saving Savannah

Claiming Charlie

Rescuing Kiera

Protecting Gabriella

Courting Isabella

ROMANTASY

-IN THE SPIRIT OF LOVE-

HISTORICAL ROMANCE

Hearts Under Fire

Wait for Me

Take Me Home

Keep Me Safe

Away Down South in Dixie

The Reluctant Bride

Stay with Me

Wanted by a Texas Ranger

KATHRYN KALEIGH

KST PUBLISHING

WANTED BY A TEXAS RANGER
PREVIEW: FINDING NATALIE

For all my Kickstarter backers,
Thank you.

I trusted a lawman over anyone else, especially the banker man sitting across from me. Probably wasn't even a banker. That would explain the hat, actually. No self-respecting banker would wear a boiler hat like that.

Standing outside the stagecoach, Captain Roberts stashed the footstool.

Glancing down at the ground, I said. "I need that—"

Without any warning, Captain Roberts put his hands on my waist and pulled me from the stagecoach. I grabbed hold of his shoulders and let a sound somewhere between an oomph and a squeal.

My skirts swirled around me as he turned and gently set me on my feet.

Wanted by a Texas Ranger

One

Grace LaCroix

May 1858

I had been sixteen the last time I had ridden in a stagecoach. Either my memory was faulty or stagecoaches had gotten much bumpier sometime during the last five years.

One of the wheels hit a bump and I nearly slid into the man sitting next to me. Wouldn't be the first time.

How he managed to sit tall and ramrod straight during this bumpy ride was beyond me. A reticent, formal man, he hadn't said a word to me since he'd joined us on the stage at our last stop nearly two hours ago. The man did not even answer direct questions. The most reaction I had seen from him was a lift of his narrow brows.

A banker, I decided, basing my opinion on his dark suit and matching boiler hat. He would have gone unnoticed back East in one of the cities, but out here in west Texas, he stood out like a sore thumb.

In the week since we had left Memphis, heading toward Tucson, Arizona, I had become accustomed to seeing cowboys wearing long dusters and bandanas to keep the grit out of their lungs. Most of the cowboys didn't bother to shave and I hadn't seen one yet who couldn't use a haircut.

In contrast to Mr. Silent Banker, the heavy-set woman, Mrs. Flora something or other, sitting across from me took up the slack for keeping up a running monologue of absolutely nothing.

"Have you ever seen a cactus shaped like that?" she asked. "I've seen drawings, but I didn't think they were real. They look like a man standing there with his arms up."

"A deformed man," I said. Most men did not have one arm several feet higher than the other.

"Yes," Flora said, brightly. "Exactly."

I hadn't really meant to encourage her, but sometimes I couldn't resist. Besides, carrying on an inane conversation while miserable was better than sitting in silence in misery.

"Look how the sun is starting to set. Have you ever seen the sun so bright?"

I shook my head. During the two days I'd ridden with Flora, I had determined that it was best to just agree with her and let her go on.

I'd also learned that if I pretended to nap, she would sit in silence.

Unfortunately, it was impossible to pretend to sleep while sliding along the seat, right into Mr. Silent Banker.

They both had handles to hold onto. Somehow I had taken the one seat that had no handle. I held onto my seat as best I could, but my wide, long skirts make that difficult.

"How much longer before our next stop?" Flora asked.

"I hope it isn't much longer," I said.

"I certainly hope it's soon," she said. "I know it's only been two hours, but with all this bouncing up and down…"

"If we stop, we'll be that much longer getting there," Mr. Silent Banker said.

Flora and I both stared at him in something akin to shock.

He'd been listening in silence to everything Flora had been saying for two hours and now he decides to say something.

I agreed with him completely. I also knew that Flora needed to use the privy. She needed to stop every two hours. Three hours was a stretch for her. She wouldn't say it outright in front of Mr. Previously Silent Banker, but she didn't have to.

With Flora thrown into a stunned silence, I turned and moved the shade aside to look out my window.

The land that never ended was dotted with those deformed cacti and tumbleweeds that made the whole landscape look desolate and depressing. It was bad enough to be able to see all the way to the horizon without a single familiar looking tree, but there was nothing. Just nothing. No houses. No fences. No people.

As I looked out toward the endless horizon, waves of heat rising and falling like waves in the ocean, I wondered if perhaps I had made a bad decision.

I had spent the last year in Memphis, working as a waitress at a café, saving every dime I could. Even though it had been tempting to buy myself a nice, fashionable dress with some of my earnings, I had refrained. Instead wearing the ones Daphne gave me. It was convenient that she and I were practically the same size. We had even been mistaken for sisters.

My friend and former employer, Daphne, had urged me to go with her to Boston.

But I didn't want to spend my best years watching Daphne starting a new life with her new husband.

I loved Daphne like a little sister, but if I had gone with them, I would still be helping her get dressed and doing her hair.

Not that I minded doing it, but there were times when I wanted to be the one wearing the pretty dress.

Honest work. Work I enjoyed.

But I knew I would spend my days helping her live her life while my own passed me by.

So I had made the decision to go my own way. The opposite way.

I was on my way to Arizona.

They said Spring was the best time to head west. I listened and I learned. Some of the customers who came into the café had been west and knew what they were talking about. Those were the ones I listened to.

Oregon was too far and it rained too much. Not only that, but if I went to Oregon, I would have to travel by wagon. Traveling by wagon was too daunting for a lady traveling alone. You had to not only buy a wagon, but horses. You have to buy food for the horses and take enough food to last for months. And water.

Arizona, with its stagecoach route, seemed like the best option. There were inns along the way and I wasn't required to bring my own provisions.

Unfortunately having a stagecoach route did not mean that they had the roads to support such travel.

As we traveled through the desert with the deformed man-looking cacti, I thought about the city life that I had given up for the sake of adventure and autonomy.

There were plenty of places I could have gone. New Orleans. Charlotte. New York, even.

But I had wanted something different.

It hadn't helped that my landlady left dime novels lying around in the parlor of the boarding house.

The dime novels made the west seem exciting and beautiful.

Instead, so far I had seen nothing much more than potholes and deformed cacti. Besides, of course, a man who could go for hours without talking and a lady who could barely let a second pass without filling it with chatter.

It would have been better if Daphne had been here.

The stagecoach slowed and Flora let out a sigh of relief.

"It's too soon," No longer silent banker man said.

"Too soon for what?" I asked.

His blank countenance looked concerned and that worried me.

I looked at Flora to see if she noticed anything, but she was focused on gathering up her skirts to bolt out the door.

I was thinking maybe I would stay inside the coach this time. But the last time I'd done that, I had regretted it. My legs were used to that every two-hour stretch. And that just happened to be the time the driver hadn't stopped for the next three hours. So after sitting for five hours, I had learned my lesson.

I would get out even though I really didn't want to.

The stagecoach came to a sudden stop. Normally one of the drivers came around to open the door and put a step down for us, but instead, they stayed on the coach. I knew because it didn't sway as it usually did.

And there were voices. Men's voices.

And they didn't sound any too friendly.

"Too soon," Mr. Banker said.

"Oh Dear," Flora said, gazing out the window. "There's nothing here."

"What do you mean?" I asked.

"There's nothing," she said. "No waystation. Anything on your side?"

I looked out my own window and saw the exact same thing.

Nothing.

We had stopped in the middle of nowhere.

The stagecoach never stopped in the middle of nowhere. It wasn't safe. The driver had explained that to Flora and basically had to remind her every time we stopped, especially after those three-hour intervals between stops.

But here we were. Stopped in the middle of nowhere.

This could not be good.

Two

Lucas Roberts

The dusty road was full of potholes created by rainstorms that were no more than a distant memory.

It hadn't rained in God knows how long and when it did, the moisture evaporated almost before it even hit the ground.

My dapple-gray horse named Sparky deftly navigated the potholes without complaint.

I had three men riding behind me. Deputies. I didn't know much about them, but we would doubtless be getting to know each other well on this particular mission.

We had been following the stagecoach for two hours.

The man we were looking for was on board. He went by the name John Blakely. We could have stopped him back at the last waystation before he boarded the stagecoach, but we needed him. We needed him to draw out the rest of his gang.

It was risky, of course. There were two women on board the stagecoach.

I had already decided that I was going to get those women off before the stage made it to the next waystation.

All the information I had, granted it wasn't much, but it was what I had to go on, pointed to John Blakely meeting up with his men at Miller's Creek.

The Blakely Gang was not known for their compassion, not even toward women. I didn't even like the idea of John Blakely being on the stagecoach with two women, but with two women and two drivers, surely Blakely would behave himself.

When Miller's Creek was about three miles away, I pulled my bandana over my nose and mouth and held up a hand to indicate to my men that they were to follow.

Nudging Sparky into a gallop, I raced toward the stagecoach. My men followed. Four galloping horses made a good bit of noise. Fortunately, the stagecoach made even more noise. They wouldn't know we were behind them until we were right up on them.

It made me sick that there were two innocent women and two innocent drivers who didn't know they were riding with an outlaw toward more outlaws.

Sparky dodged a tumbleweed and in the process barely missed landing in one of the potholes.

The last thing I needed was to lose a horse out here.

But fortunately Sparky was a good horse. Been with me a long time. Since West Point. He had a lot of miles on him. Or I should say we had a lot of miles under us.

I slowed enough for my men to catch up as we reached the stagecoach.

I went around to the left of the stagecoach while my men stayed behind.

The driver looked startled to see me. Things happened when people got complacent out here. If nothing else, this would put them back on alertness where they should be.

Not only was the Blakely Gang out here, but the Comanches were fighting back. Couldn't blame them. Settlers were taking over their hunting grounds.

Fortunately, they left the stagecoaches alone for the most part.

Riding close to the driver, I held up my badge.

"Need you to stop the coach," I said. "Don't make a ruckus."

"Yes sir," the driver said, pulling on the reins.

The stagecoach slowed, then came to a rather abrupt stop.

"Stay there," I said.

My men were positioned just behind the stagecoach waiting for my signal.

They knew what our mission was.

Get the women out of the stagecoach, then two of us would be boarding the coach with Mr. Blakely.

The goal was to blend in and pretend to be just normal stage-coach passengers.

Too bad I hadn't found out about the two women on board until after the stagecoach had already left town. This would have looked a lot less fishy.

Falling back, I dismounted and tossed my reins to the one we called "The Kid."

He would be one of the two men taking the women back to wait for the next stagecoach.

If only everything went smoothly. Hopefully it wasn't too much to ask.

We were due for some good luck. Overdue.

Three

GRACE

I let the leather window covering fall back into place. With it open, dust floated inside the coach even more so than with it closed.

Even Flora lowered her window covering as we came to a stop and the dust pooled around the coach.

She put a hand on the doorknob to open the door.

"Flora," I said, warning in my voice. I shook my head quickly when she looked at me.

She released the door handle and sat back. Her eyes were wide with alarm.

Mr. No Longer Silent Banker banged on the front of the coach.

"Why have we stopped?" he demanded to know.

No one answered.

The three of us sat in silence. Flora's eyes were wide with fear as she watched the door. Mr. Banker silently fumed with anger. I could see the anger practically coming out of his ears.

I sat warily. Instead of watching the door, though, I peeked outside the window.

Dust be damned.

I was soon rewarded with catching sight of two men dismounting and tying their horses to the back of the stagecoach.

The men didn't look like cowboys and they didn't look like outlaws. They looked like lawmen to me.

"What do you see?" Flora asked, her voice shaky.

"Nothing," I said, letting the leather curtain fall back into place.

Mr. Silent Again Banker watched me warily.

He obviously did not believe me. Flora didn't believe me either, but that didn't concern me. What did concern me was that Mr. Banker cared one way or the other.

Something wasn't right with him.

I wasn't sure what it was just yet, but there was something off. Maybe it was his eyes. Or his silence. Probably his hat.

No self-respecting gentleman wore a hat like that.

The door opened and a man stood there, leaning casually against the door frame as though he didn't have a care in the world.

"Good afternoon Ladies and Gentleman." He dipped his hat to Flora, then me, but his attention was on Mr. Angry Banker.

"What is the meaning of this?" Mr. Banker said.

"No need for you to worry, Sir," he said. "I'm here to retrieve the ladies. You're free to go on your way as soon as I have them off the coach."

"Oh dear," Flora said. "It's the Indians, isn't it? I'm going to need my smelling salts."

"No need to fear, ma'am," the lawman without a visible badge said.

Even though I couldn't see his badge, I knew he was a lawman.

He looked different from the other men—the cowboys, the drivers, even the banker. Calm. In charge. Competent.

And unlike the other men I'd seen in Texas, he had shaved. Maybe not today, but a day or so ago. It made him look so much more... civilized... and... handsome.

When his gaze met mine, I saw even more in his eyes. I saw a world of knowledge.

Or that was what I told myself. With his deep blue eyes locked on mine, I could not look away. Didn't want to look away.

His gaze wove a spell around me, leaving me feeling ungrounded.

"Where are we going?" Flora asked, breaking the spell.

"I have to take you back to town." Mr. Lawman shifted his gaze to Flora.

"Town?" Flora asked. "You mean that waystation back there?"

"Yes ma'am. Horsehead Crossing."

"Horsehead Crossing," Flora exclaimed, with a touch of hysteria coming into her voice. "That is not a town."

"It has an inn," Mr. Lawman said.

Flora crossed her arms and shook her head. "No. I'm not going back there."

Mr. Lawman looked to me for help.

I didn't know his reason for wanting to take us back to Horsehead Crossing. Personally, I hadn't thought it was all that bad. It had actually had some of the best food we'd had since we left Memphis.

But there was something to be said for solidarity.

"If she isn't going, then I'm not going either."

"For God's sake," Mr. Lawman said. "It's only temporary. We'll get you on the next stage out."

"My husband is waiting for me," Flora said. "If I'm not there, he'll leave without me. Don't think he won't. I don't have time for such a delay. Why, my husband will be halfway to Denver by the time I catch up."

"I understand," Mr. Lawman said.

I looked at Flora. Why on earth had she come this far south if she was heading to Denver?

"Why does he get to stay?" Flora asked.

Something about the look in Mr. Lawman's face. Such a subtle shift in his features that I was the only one to see it told me that Flora had just stuck her toe where it didn't belong.

"Flora," I said.

Flora was shaking her head and muttering to herself.

"Flora," I said, more loudly this time.

The older woman looked at me. "Would you rather lose a couple of days at most or would you rather be dead?"

"Dead?" Her bravado faded.

I leaned forward and lowered my voice, knowing everyone could hear me. Didn't matter. It was for effect.

"You know he's trying to protect us from Indians." I looked up to the Lawman. "Isn't that right, Mr...?"

"Roberts, ma'am. Captain Roberts."

"It's the Indians?" I needed him to say yes. I knew Flora was a strong woman. The only weakness I had discovered in two days of travel was her fear of Indians.

"Yes ma'am," Mr. Lawman agreed. "There's been an outbreak."

"Oh for God's sake," Mr. Banker said. "Just go with the man. Who cares? The stagecoach needs to be on time." He leaned forward, peering at Flora with an intensity that had her recoiling. "If the stage-coach is late, the Indians will know."

I doubted the Indians knew the stagecoach's exact schedule, but it wasn't impossible.

"Oh. Very well," Flora said. "Anything to get out of this coach."

I bit my lip to keep from smiling. Should have led with that one. Even stronger than her fear of Indians was her constant need for the privy.

She started moving forward toward the door.

Captain Roberts grabbed the footstool and allowed her to hold his hand while she got out of the stagecoach.

Blocking my way to the door, Mr. Banker watched me, his eyes narrowed. "Don't think I won't remember you."

I didn't say anything as I scooted over to the opposite seat and slid my way toward the door.

Mr. Banker seemed to think I knew what was going on. I hadn't a clue. All I knew was how to get Flora off the stagecoach.

I trusted a lawman over anyone else, especially this banker man. Probably wasn't even a banker. That would explain the hat, actually. No self-respecting banker would wear a boiler hat like that.

Captain Roberts stashed the footstool.

Glancing down at the ground, I said. "I need the—"

Without any warning, Captain Roberts put his hands on my waist and pulled me from the stagecoach. I grabbed hold of his shoulders and let a sound somewhere between an oomph and a squeal.

My skirts swirled around me as he turned and gently set me on my feet.

My feet were hardly on the ground before a younger man grabbed my hand and pulled me toward the horses tied behind the stagecoach.

Four

LUCAS

So much for my plans.

My plan had been to get the women off the coach and headed back in the other direction.

I had not anticipated resistance. I should have. Any self-respecting woman would have resisted getting off their stagecoach out in the middle of nowhere.

My plan had been to get them off, then climb aboard the stage and ride with Blakely.

Thanks to the older woman's resistance, I'd had to change my tactic.

The younger girl, thankfully, had been intuitive enough that she had stopped resisting and had helped me convince the older woman to get off the stagecoach.

I'd had to come up with a new plan on the fly. I'd revealed my identity as Captain Roberts. Now Blakely would be suspicious. I doubted he would buy the whole Indian attack story.

"Where's your friend?" I asked coming back from instructing the drivers to unload the ladies' trunks at the next stop in Miller's Creek.

The girl was standing next to The Kid.

"She needed a moment of privacy," the girl said.

Privacy was always a challenge out here, especially for a lady.

"I need you to ride back to Horsehead Crossing with..." I searched for The Kid's name. "Peter."

"You aren't coming with us?" she asked.

This young lady had long, dark hair, a few strands falling from the confines of the green bonnet she wore. Her dress, also green, high necked and long-sleeved, paled in comparison to her bright green eyes.

Her bow shaped lips were tipped up questioningly. Not a pout. Most girls would have pouted. But with this one, I saw no guile, no effort to get her way by batting her lashes and pouting prettily. Instead, I saw just a simple question. Maybe a little disappointment, but I could easily have imagined that.

It was a little disconcerting to acknowledge to myself that I was disappointed.

"I can't," I said. "I have responsibilities."

She nodded. Then she smiled and her whole face transformed from beautiful to more beautiful. She reminded me of a butterfly. A butterfly is beautiful with its wings closed, but with its wings open, it is even more beautiful.

Right then and there I was an inch away from forgetting all about Blakely. Letting him go ahead on his own. Responsibilities be damned.

It was, of course, a fleeting thought.

I hadn't become a Texas Ranger Captain by shirking my duties.

I had also never met this young lady whose name I didn't even know.

"Sir?" It was my second in command. "Sir? Awaiting your orders."

Drinking in one last look of the young lady in front of me, I tipped my hat to her and turned on my heel.

Duty called.

Five

GRACE

We had no more than watched Captain Lucas Roberts and one of the other Texas Rangers ride off in the stagecoach than it became evident that Flora and I did not have horses.

Even though I could have ridden on the horse along with Peter or the other man, Flora needed a horse of her own.

After conferring for about half a minute, the two men decided that Flora and I would ride their horses and they would walk.

I didn't say anything, but it seemed to me that the Texas Rangers hadn't done very much planning on this particular campaign.

After about ten minutes on the horse, Flora regained her chattiness.

"Are we in danger out here?" she asked. "From the Indians?"

"I don't think so Ma'am," Trevor said.

"I sure hope the stagecoach drivers will be okay out there. They're nice fellows. I'd hate to hear they got attacked by Indians."

The two soldiers looked at each other.

"I'm sure they will be fine, Ma'am."

I decided right then that there were no Indians. Something else was up.

Captain Lucas Roberts had boarded that stagecoach for a very good reason, but it had nothing to do with Indians.

I'd wager it had something to do with Mr. Boiler Hat. He was a shady looking man and I didn't trust him.

It bothered me that Lucas was in the stagecoach with him. But there were two of them and they were soldiers. Mr. Boiler Hat was not a match for two Texas Rangers.

I straightened on the horse's back and kept my gaze straight ahead.

I couldn't stop thinking about Lucas. He was a handsome man with sparkling blue eyes that sent my heart racing.

I glanced over my shoulder, but of course I couldn't see the stagecoach. It had already traveled out of sight.

"What happens next?" I asked Peter.

"You get a room at the inn and catch the next stagecoach west."

"What if it's full?" Flora asked.

"I guess you'll have to wait on the next one."

"I can't do that. Like I told the other ranger, my husband is waiting."

"Surely he won't really leave without you," I said.

I had to turn my head away when a gust of wind brought a new onslaught of dirt.

Peter had already pulled his bandana over his mouth and nose.

"I need one of those," I said. When I had booked on the stagecoach, I hadn't thought I would be riding outside in the desert.

Peter reached into his pocket and brought out a white bandana. Handed it to me.

"Thank you," I said. "You're very kind."

I held his bandana over my mouth when the next gust of wind hit us.

"I have never seen wind like this," Flora said. "Does it ever rain out here?"

"Yes ma'am."

I smiled to myself. It was rather nice to have someone else for Flora to talk to.

While she rattled on, I let my thoughts wander and didn't even have to feign sleep.

My thoughts went right straight to Lucas.

All I knew about Captain Lucas Roberts was his name and that he was a Texas Rangers Captain.

Somehow it was enough.

I had learned over the years to be very practical. To keep my thoughts to myself for the most part. I had been Daphne's lady's maid for five years. A lady's maid's job was not to impose her opinion on anything outside of fashion. And even then, a lady's maid had to tread carefully.

Of course, I had not adhered to those rules. Daphne and I were too close in age for me not to share my opinions with her on several occasions.

She had made a good match with Ambrose. The two of them had grown up together, always crushing on each other, but not realizing it was reciprocated.

They had fallen in love with a slow burn. That was a good way to fall in love, I suppose. But I had never had that opportunity.

For me, there just might be another way of falling in love.

Sometimes love came over a person in a flash.

I'd heard about that sort of thing. Never put much stock in it, but maybe, just maybe there was something to it.

"Yes ma'am," Trevor said, catching my attention back to their conversation. "Captain Roberts will be joining us after he finishes his mission."

Thank you, Flora for asking the very question I really, really wanted an answer to.

I would be seeing Captain Roberts again.

Six

LUCAS

For the next three miles, all my attention stayed on Blakely.

The stagecoach moved along, covering the distance, the driver hitting every pothole in the dirt road. Dirt wove its way inside past the leather flaps that served as curtains.

Matthew and I stayed calm and collected, at least in appearance. But both of us were on high alert.

We watched Blakely's every move. The man was most definitely in disguise. A boiler hat? Really?

No one would certainly ever mistake him for an outlaw. Not dressed like this.

I'd never met the man, but I could see the evil in his eyes. It was there when he looked at me, his unblinking black eyes piercing into mine.

He was not a man I wanted to meet on the street, much less cross. Right now, though, Matthew and I had the advantage. We knew he was Blakely, the outlaw, but he didn't know we knew.

He knew we knew something, but he didn't know what it was.

As the coach slowed, he pulled out a silver pocket watch that was so shiny it looked like a mirror. After he checked the time, he slid it back into his jacket pocket.

The coach rolled into Miller's Creek and stopped in the middle of the road between the inn and the barn. The rest of the town, if you could call it that was half a mile up ahead.

There was nothing else to see here. Just a two-story house that served as an inn—one room on the first floor that the owner let out when needed. The barn was really nothing more than a one-room building with a hayloft. An area out back for horses. There was currently one horse, standing outside flicking his tail at whatever insect happened to be bothering him. Probably a horsefly.

The drivers, who would typically start throwing trunks off the top of the stagecoach sat there, not moving.

So much for not looking suspicious.

I opened the stagecoach door and hopped out.

Miller's Creek was a waystation. A place to water the horses and feed the passengers. Just a room for an overnight stay if someone needed it.

It did have one thing that most of the other waystations along the way did not have.

It had a General Store and a Church.

Blakely and his men were after the General Store.

In these parts, a General Store played the role of a bank. The only place around here to send a letter. And the only place that had any money.

Next best thing to a bank.

It fit the Blakely Gang just perfectly.

They rolled into town, under disguise, like Blakely now, looking like some kind of dandy with his boiler hat.

The man really needed to work on his disguises.

But with any luck, he would be behind bars after today. The one thing Miller's Creek did not have that would be nice was a jail.

Since they didn't have a jail, that meant we had to haul them back to Horsehead Crossing where they did have a jail, of sorts, and a judge who came through every month or so.

Once I got them to the jail, they were no longer my problem.

"Go ahead," I said to the driver. "Do what you normally do."

The driver saluted me and proceeded to toss Blakely's one trunk off the top of the stagecoach. When it hit the ground, it tossed up a heap of dust and the damn thing popped open.

Empty. It was empty.

The trunk was just another prop. Like Blakely's boiler's hat.

This thing was going down and it was going down quick. Quicker than we had planned.

Well. The sooner we got it over with, the sooner I could get back to Horsehead Crossing.

And the sooner I could see the girl again.

I should have gotten her name. How could a man meet an angel like that and not at least get her name?

I had been smitten, that was how. Too smitten to even think about getting her name.

Well, once I got back to Horsehead Crossing, that was the first thing I was going to do. I was going to get the girl's name.

But right now, if I didn't stay focused we were going to have a gunfight.

Stay focused.

That was my only job right now.

Seven

GRACE

Sitting in an oversized high back wooden chair at the sturdy wooden table that would easily hold eight people, I scooped a big spoonful of mashed potatoes onto my plate. The china plate looked out of place here in the middle of nowhere somewhere in west Texas on this big, chunky wooden table.

Horsehead Crossing had an inn and like all the waystations had a well with fresh water.

The proprietors obviously had not planned on us returning so soon after leaving this morning. Last night we had baked fish. No baked fish tonight. Instead, we were having mashed potatoes, baked beans, and slabs of ham.

The fish had been a welcome treat that had reminded me of the home where I had lived with Daphne and her family. The one place I actually considered home. The place where my mother was buried. That probably had a lot to do with why I thought of it as home.

Nonetheless, the ham tasted like it had been smoked over a fire pit. Since there weren't any trees out here to chop down for firewood,

I could only think that they'd had it delivered in. Had to have firewood shipped in, too.

"Do you know when the next stage coach is coming through?" Flora asked the older couple, the Parkers, who owned the inn. She'd already asked them four times since we had gotten here an hour ago.

"Should be in a couple of days." Mrs. Parker said. She was undoubtedly a patient woman, answering Flora's questions and carrying on a conversation that made no sense. Flora would make a comment, then change the subject with no transition, whatsoever.

Truly, she was hard to keep up with. I had a slight advantage over most people. First I had spent the last year working as a waitress in a very busy café in Memphis and second I had spent the five years before that working as a lady's maid in the Amirault household.

Working as a waitress had taught me to hold several different conversations with several different people as I went back and forth to the tables.

Working as a lady's maid was significant in that the Amiraults had five children as did their neighbors, the Beausejours. The two families were quite close and with ten children between them, there was always, always some kind of activity going on even on a lazy Sunday afternoon.

So Flora didn't bother me. I could follow four conversations at one time. In fact, I could not only follow those four conversations, but I was fairly certain I could follow at least one of them in French. This was, of course, untested. And would probably remain that way. It seemed the further west I traveled, the less opportunity there was going to be for me to hear anyone speaking in French.

"Captain Lucas has been through here several times. A very good man," Mrs. Parker was saying.

Hearing Captain Lucas's name snagged my attention. I focused on her, hanging on her every word.

"None of the Rangers who come through here are married. Unfortunately, they're away from home too much to have a family."

"That's a pity," Flora said, shaking her head and making a little tsking sound.

I couldn't agree more. However, if that meant Captain Lucas was unmarried, then perhaps that wasn't such a bad thing.

In fact, I was quite certain it was a good thing.

"Would you like some more potatoes, Dear?" Mrs. Parker asked, noticing that I had cleaned my plate.

"Yes," I said. "I would. Thank you."

She passed the plate of mashed potatoes over and I took a spoonful.

Flora looked at me without comment—something quite unusual for her.

I just shrugged. With the exception of the fish last night at this very inn, I had eaten very little in the two days we had traveled together.

My dress was hanging a little loose and I was constantly hungry, but the food we'd been given to eat along the way had done little to stir the appetite.

I had a feeling it wasn't just that the mashed potatoes were quite good. It was that I was feeling a little bit almost giddy.

This was turning out to be a very good day.

Eight

LUCAS

This was turning out to be a very bad day.

We had followed John Blakely to the inn. Sat through a supper that left a lot to be desired—some kind of watery stew with unknown ingredients—and still there was no sign that he was meeting up with any of his gang members.

I was beginning to think that our intel was wrong.

That distinct possibility annoyed me quite a bit. Instead of being here with Matthew keeping an eye on John Blakely, I could be at Horsehead Crossing with the girl.

As I bit into a dried out biscuit, I reminded myself that if it had not been for Blakely, I would not have met the girl at all.

That reminder did nothing to alleviate my annoyance.

Matthew, sitting next to me, leaned close. "What do we do now?"

"Wait," I said. It was all we could do. Just sit keeping an eye on Blakely with his boiler hat on the table next to him while he pretended not to know that we were watching him.

I would not be surprised to learn that he was dragging his feet on meeting up with his gang just to irritate us.

It was working.

Finally, after taking his time with a leisurely meal, Blakely pushed back his chair and slowly put his boiler hat on his head.

Matthew and I went on alert.

Finally the man was going to do something besides sit here. I slid a hand over the pistol at my hip, hidden beneath my trench coat.

My time with the Rangers was up if I wanted it to be. I could choose to stay in or I could choose to get out and do something else with my life.

I'd always figured I'd make a career out of being a Texas Ranger. But lately I'd been feeling restless. Itchy even. I couldn't shake the feeling that there had to be something else. Something I was missing.

Blakely looked around, met my gaze, and he grinned.

I was a tough enough man, and there wasn't much that scared me these days, but seeing a grin on Blakely's face was enough to make a strong man recoil. If not with fear, then with trepidation at least.

Then Blakely turned around and instead of leaving the inn's dining room, he went upstairs.

Matthew groaned.

"Looks like we're in for a long night," I said. "Go get some rest. I'll take the first watch."

Matthew, a seasoned ranger like myself, nodded, and stood up.

"I'll be back in three hours," he said. "Unless you need me."

"If I need you, I'll let you know," I said.

I went over to the black pot-bellied stove and refilled my tin cup with hot coffee.

The innkeepers had gone to bed an hour ago, leaving us to take care of ourselves.

It was going to be a long night.

Either we were going to sit here all night and wait for nothing or Blakely was going to try to make his move under the cover of darkness.

Either way, it was most definitely going to be a long night.

Adding a lump of sugar into my coffee just for the hell of it, because I could, I stirred my coffee and took it back to my chair.

One thing about it. I was going to have plenty of time to think.

And, it seemed, I had quite a bit to think about.

Nine

GRACE

I woke in the night disoriented.

It was pitch dark without a stitch of moonlight coming through the window—if there even was a window. I lay there on the lumpy mattress, giving myself time to figure out where I was.

It all clicked when I realized that sound I was hearing was Flora snoring. That was the thing with these inns, they usually only had one bed sometimes two if we were lucky. Men and women had to stay in separate rooms, but other than that, there was little to no privacy.

One point in favor of traveling west in a wagon.

If I'd had a husband, traveling west in a wagon would probably have been the best option. But not for a woman traveling alone. Hooking up wagons to horses and such. Having to drive a wagon at all, much less across dangerous rivers. I wasn't built that way.

I might have worked as a lady's maid due to circumstances outside of my control, but I had been born and bred a lady.

I distinctly remembered growing up in a happy home until that fateful day when I turned six years old. My father had been run down by a carriage. We had been home at the time the news came. I had been sitting at my desk, my legs swinging, translating Latin. I'd never touched Latin again after that day.

My mother had held on as long as she could. She made it for five years, but our house had been much too large and the money had been depleted quickly without my father's lucrative business income. Then the bank had come for the house.

At the end of her rope, my mother had responded to an advertisement to work as a lady's maid in northern Louisiana. Our lives had never been the same.

I had never even driven a wagon. As an adult, whenever I went somewhere I had traveled with Daphne and she certainly didn't drive her own wagon. She did, however, ride a horse and ride quite well.

I knew fashion and could speak French, but I'd never had the opportunity to learn to ride a horse. Daphne had threatened to teach me on several occasions, but I had managed to avoid it.

At any rate, sleeping in a bed with a snoring woman was a lot less daunting than navigating the west in my own wagon. And to be honest, I didn't know anything about horses. Or cooking. Or shooting a gun for that matter. All things required of traveling west.

As I lay there listening to Flora snore and a dog or a wolf howling somewhere in the distance, I contemplated my life.

I had arrived with my mother at the Amirault's home. Mama had worked as an indentured servant. But she had passed away shortly after we got there. The Amiraults had taken me in, taken care of me, and in return I went to work as Daphne's lady's maid. That had been an interesting transition, but the family was kind and gave me plenty of time to learn what I was supposed to do.

Daphne and I had gone from child to adults together.

Then when Daphne had run off to Memphis, I had gone with her.

That's when I really began to make my own choices. I'd chosen to stay in Memphis when Daphne had moved to Boston with her new husband. Then, after saving my money, I had decided to take the Butterfield Stagecoach west to Tucson.

And here I was. Somewhere in the middle of nowhere in the middle of that journey.

Just this morning, I had been doubting my choice to come west.

And I probably would continue to do so until I got to Tucson and got settled in.

But at the moment, I was feeling a little bit happy about my choice.

Even though things were a little uncertain right now, and I had been forced to retrace a day's travel, I was optimistic.

I had never had a beau. Being a lady's maid was not conducive to romance. I purposely avoided both the Amirault and the Beausejour brothers simply because I knew about the complications that could create. I was the help and they were the employers.

There was no one else.

But now I had met Lucas, a Texas Ranger who had me feeling lightheaded just thinking about him. It was an odd sensation, being around him.

But I liked it.

I liked it that I was free to look into a man's eyes and allow my feelings to surface.

Lucas was a handsome, rugged man whose lifestyle, according to everyone, was not conducive to having a family. I wasn't looking to have a family either, at least not until I got to Tucson.

That didn't stop the butterflies in my stomach.

There were some things a woman could not control. And there were some things a woman did not want to control.

I could think of far worse fates than falling head over heels for a Texas Ranger.

Ten

LUCAS

Just after the break of dawn, with the sun announcing its impending arrival by splashing reds and pinks, and pale yellows across the horizon, I sat outside the little house that served as an inn with Matthew.

We sat in two wooden chairs covered in a sheen of dust. Everything was covered with dust out here. It floated in the air itself.

"He didn't come down," Matthew said.

I slapped my gloves against my thigh. Running off of three hours of sleep.

A rooster crowing across the street fluttered its wings, feathers going everywhere, and flew aside when an old dog ran up, yipping at it. A farmer rumbled along in his wagon, probably heading out to his fields.

Just a small community out in the middle of nowhere.

"He's not coming down," I said.

Matthew leaned forward. Looked at me like I had just sprouted horns.

"What makes you say that?"

"How much do you want to bet?" I asked, lifting my hat and running a hand through my hair.

"I'm not betting against you." Matthew sat back, shaking his head.

"Smart move," I said.

"So you say he's not coming down? What the hell?"

"We'll go up there, kick in his door, and the room will be empty."

"Son of a—" Matthew tipped his chair onto its two back legs. "He went out the back."

"Come on," I said. "Let's go up there and confirm my brilliance."

"Anything to get out of this hell hole," he said.

"I guess you'd rather be out there sleeping on the ground," I said, holding the door for him.

We stepped inside the relative coolness of the inn. To the scent of biscuits baking and what hopefully was bacon frying. My stomach grumbled in hopefulness. After last night's questionable fare, I was looking forward something resembling normal food.

I went upstairs first. I was the one in command, after all. And I was the one who knew Blakely. I'd followed him. I'd studied him.

I threw open the unlocked door.

And now I had lost him.

"Son of a—" Matthew slammed his fist against the door frame.

"Don't take it personal," I said. "I should have seen it coming."

"Yeah, well. Neither one of us did." Matthew went to the open window. Looked down. "That man did not jump from here."

"He had help," I said flatly. "They were here. They were waiting for him. And he escaped right under our nose."

"Do we go look for him?" Matthew asked. "The General Store?"

"He's long gone," I said, picking up the boiler hat Blakely had left on the dresser. "I hope he picks a better disguise next time."

Matthew let out a laugh. "Damn. I was hoping there wouldn't be a next time."

"Me too." I set the hat back on the dresser. "Me too."

"So we don't follow?"

"Nah. Give him time to surface again. Let him think he's lost us."

"He has," Matthew said.

"Just keep telling yourself that," I said. "That's the thing about Blakely. He always shows up."

"We'll head to Cactus Rock, then? Join the other rangers?"

"You go ahead. I have something I need to take care of."

"Suit yourself."

I wouldn't tell Matthew this, but I was more than happy to throw this whole thing in and head back to Horsehead Crossing.

There was a girl there whose name I needed to get.

And that, as far as I was concerned, was more important than anything Blakely might be doing.

Eleven

GRACE

I was surprised to find a little river about a half mile from town. Compared to the Mississippi River, though, it was no more than a rivulet. A man with a strong arm could probably throw a rock across it and hit what passed as a tree on the other side.

I had walked here and sat on the edge of the water mostly so I wouldn't keep looking down the road for Captain Lucas Roberts.

It was quite likely that I would be on the next stagecoach out of here before he came back to Horsehead Crossing. I *knew* that, but it didn't keep me from wanting to see him again.

It wasn't his fault that he held the burden of being my first real crush. Or at least the first one I had allowed myself to acknowledge. I hadn't even told him my name. Unless Flora had told him, and I didn't think she had, he didn't know it.

It was a flight of fancy to think about seeing him again. So I watched a limb drifting along in the slow current until it was out of sight and thought about something else.

The water was too murky to see below the surface. I tried to imagine riding a horse across that water, but it was too much. My mind couldn't begin to fathom it.

The next stagecoach was supposed to be coming through later today or maybe in the morning. There was no guarantee there would be space on it. I hoped that there was space and I hoped it came soon.

I managed to not think about Lucas for all of two seconds.

Other than wanting to see Lucas again, I was ready to move. I was ready to get to Tucson. To be somewhere.

I wanted roots. Roots of my own.

I got to my feet and dusted off my skirts before turning around, ready to head back to the inn. Maybe I could look around and find a book to read.

Captain Lucas Roberts was standing behind me, holding his hat in one hand.

"Good morning," he said.

"You're not supposed to be here yet."

"When am I supposed to be here?" he asked with a curious little grin.

"I don't know," I said, my line of thinking faltering. "Just not now. So soon."

"I couldn't wait any longer. I have something very important I need to find the answer to."

"So you had to come back here to find out the answer to a question."

"That's right," he said.

"What? What is it you need to know?"

"It's simple really. What is your name?"

"Grace," I said without hesitation.

He grinned. "That's perfect. It fits you perfectly."

"Thank you," I said, looking at him dubiously.

"What's your last name?"

"LaCroix."

"French. You don't sound French."

"I have some French blood back there somewhere."

"Where are you from?"

"Philadelphia," I said, crossing my arms. "Am I in some kind of trouble?"

"Of course not."

"You ask a lot of questions."

"Yes. Well. I had a lot of time to think. And I had to know your name so I could think of you by name instead of just that pretty girl from the stagecoach."

My heart stuttered.

"You think I'm pretty?"

"You are pretty."

"No one has ever told me that before."

"Please tell me you're kidding."

"No." I shook my head.

"Well that is just a pity. You should be told how pretty you are several times every day."

"Well, that's an unusual way of thinking."

"I see nothing unusual about making sure a pretty girl knows just how pretty she is."

I didn't know what to say, so I said nothing.

"Are you about to walk back? Can I walk with you?"

"Sure." I took the arm he offered, tucking my hand in the crook of his elbow. "Did you take care of whatever it was you were trying to do?"

"Not really," he said. "He got away."

I stopped and looked up at him. "It was him, wasn't it? It was that man wearing that awful hat."

"That man in the awful hat is the outlaw John Blakely."

"I've heard of him. I knew there was something wrong about that man."

"How did you know?" he asked. We started walking again. The inn was just up ahead. Light smoke curled out from the chimney.

"Just a gut feeling. He didn't say much. That was probably it. He was decidedly unfriendly. But it was probably his hat."

Lucas laughed. "I agree. The worst hat. But he is not known for his compassion, especially toward women."

"So it wasn't Indians at all?"

"Not this time. We were trying not reveal ourselves as Texas Rangers to him."

"Well," I said. "I would think that would be almost impossible to do."

"Why is that?"

"I don't know," I said. "You're not like other men."

"Is this supposed to be a compliment?"

"You can take it that way," I said, with a little shrug.

"I will then. Thank you."

We slowed as we neared the inn.

"So what now? Do you go after him again?"

"Maybe later. Right now we really do have Indians to take care of."

My heart sank. That meant he would not be here for long.

"Come on in here," Mrs. Parker said, coming to the door. "Dinner is ready."

"Looks like we're just in time," he said.

"So it seems."

We followed Mrs. Parker inside to sit at the dining table.

Flora was already there eating fish. We were having fish again.

Lucas held my chair as I sat down across from her and then he sat down next to me.

This was a most interesting turn of events.

Twelve

LUCAS

I sat next to Miss Grace LaCroix at the Parker's big dining room table while Mrs. Parker brought out a platter of baked fish.

Mrs. Parker and Flora chattered on about absolutely nothing. Grace glanced over at me and I smiled. She quickly looked away. But neither of the older women were paying us any mind.

"Mr. Parker is out with the horses," Mrs. Parker said as though implying that I, too, should be outside helping in the barn.

"I'm sorry he has to miss out on such a fine dinner," I said, taking my fork and placing a slice of fish on Grace's plate, then I put one on mine.

"Well," Mrs. Parker said. "I'll save him some, of course."

"I would expect nothing less. Did Mr. Parker catch these fish?"

"He certainly did," Mrs. Parker said with obvious pride. "He was up fishing before sunrise."

I didn't see how a man could fish in the dark. But since I didn't fish, I wasn't one to question.

"Did you find that nasty man from the stagecoach?" Flora asked.

"No," I said.

"There was something about him that I didn't like." Flora kept talking before I had time to elaborate. It was just as well. I really didn't want Blakely to be the topic of our dinner conversation.

I cleaned my plate before I realized Grace hadn't eaten much.

"Is everything to your liking?" I leaned over to ask her.

"Of course," she said. "The fish is excellent."

"She doesn't eat much," Flora said, boldly jumping into our conversation. "You can tell by how skinny she is."

"I ate yesterday," Grace said, shifting uncomfortably in her chair.

"It's okay," I said. "You don't have to eat if you don't want to."

"I have a fresh apple pie," Mrs. Parker said brightly.

"Where did you get fresh apples?" Grace asked.

"We have people coming through here all the time. They run the stagecoach route, knowing that we're going to need lots of supplies."

"That makes sense," Grace said.

"I'll take a slice of pie," Flora said.

"There's plenty to go around," Mrs. Parker said. "No need for anyone to be shy."

While Mrs. Parker sliced the pie, my gaze locked with Grace's. Her cheeks were flushed as she looked at me with those bright green eyes. Her eyes mesmerized me, making it hard to look away.

Mrs. Parker handed me a plate with a slice of pie and I handed it over to Grace. Our fingers brushed and her cheeks flushed a little more.

I grinned, taking heart that it was possible she liked me too.

"When do you think we'll be leaving for Miller's Creek?" Flora asked.

"You should be on the next stagecoach," I said.

Flora swept a hand in a general direction toward nothing. "Well," she said. "There's something you people failed to take into consideration."

"What's that ma'am?"

"Our trunks are in Miller's Creek. And we are here. That is a problem."

I looked over at Grace. She was wearing the same green dress she had been wearing yesterday.

"You're right," I said. "That is something of a problem."

Thirteen

GRACE

The fresh apple pie was stunningly good, reaffirming my opinion that the best food on this stagecoach route was right here at Horsehead Crossing.

It was so good that I ate the whole piece, despite my nerves being on edge from sitting next to Lucas.

He was a big man. At least a head taller than me. With him sitting next to me, I felt safe. Blakely himself could have barged in through the front door and I was confident that Lucas would have things under control.

Maybe it was because I knew he was a Texas Ranger. He didn't look so much like a Ranger right now. His clothes, like mine, were the same that he had been wearing yesterday and he still had not shaved.

I couldn't possibly know what he had been doing since I saw him last. Since he pulled me from the stagecoach and sent me away. But I could only imagine that he hadn't had time for such things as shaving.

He had come straight here. He had come straight here in order to learn my name.

So he had been thinking about me, too. Either that or he was one of those suave, charming men with a silver tongue. I shook my head. No. That didn't fit him. He didn't seem like a rogue at all. I'd seen enough rogues when I had lived with the Amiraults as a lady's maid to know one when I saw him.

"What are you thinking about?" Lucas asked.

"Nothing," I said with a little smile.

He looked at me sideways. "Nothing, huh?"

"Nothing," I said with a little secret smile.

Lucas was definitely not a rogue. And, I realized with a start, it wouldn't matter if he was.

I had already fallen under his spell.

A rumbling outside had all of us looking toward the door.

"What's that?" Flora asked.

I knew exactly what it was.

"It's the stagecoach," Lucas said, looking none too happy.

"Thank the Good Lord," Flora said, fanning her face and getting up to go to the door.

Mrs. Parker followed along behind her, the two ladies chattering about something.

I set my fork on top of my plate and pushed it away.

After wishing for the stagecoach to hurry and arrive, now that it had, I wished for it to go away.

As much as I wanted to get to Tucson, I wanted to stay with Lucas more.

This did not bode well for me.

"This is good news," Lucas said. "You can continue your trip now."

"Yes," I said. "Good news.

"Right. We should go see how many seats they have available."

"Yes," I said. "We should do that."

But we both just sat there. Listening to the commotion outside. People shouting. Dogs barking. Normal sounds of a stagecoach's arrival.

And yet, there was nothing normal about this moment.

Fourteen

LUCAS

The stagecoach was here and Grace was going to have to leave soon.

Despite what I said out loud, this was not good news. Not good news at all. I had planned on spending some time with Grace.

During the long hours I had spent sitting at the inn in Miller's Creek watching for Blakely to come down the stairs, guns blazing, I had given a lot of thought to my life.

I had reassessed my choices looking at them from a new perspective. The perspective of a man on the precipice of thirty.

I'd made my mark with the Texas Rangers. Now younger men, like the Kid, were coming in. I had more experience, but the Kid had more bravado and as much as I didn't like to admit, bravado was a big part of what made a Texas Ranger who he was.

It was time for me to move up in the ranks. Maybe even take a desk job. Be a commander.

The conclusion I had come to when I had been sitting in that little inn, alone, in the shadows, was that, even though it was the natural order of things, it wasn't what I wanted to do.

I was ready for something new. Something different.

It was time for me to go to the next chapter in my life.

With the ruckus of the arriving stagecoach in the background, I watched Grace.

She was staring straight ahead, toward the door, but wasn't making any move to get up and join them. To see how many seats were available on the stagecoach.

"Grace," I said. "Can I ask you something?"

She shifted her gaze to mine. Her deep green eyes were unfathomable. I wanted to read her thoughts. To know what she was thinking. But she was a mystery to me. A mystery I wanted to solve, but I had a feeling I never would. She was far too complex.

"Okay."

"You're headed to Tucson?"

"Yes."

"Why?"

She tilted her head and looked at me, not answering.

"Why Tucson?" I asked again, stacking my own plate next to hers.

"Because it's where the stagecoach goes."

"That sounds like something a man would say."

"Does it?" She smiled.

"But seriously?" I asked. "Do you have family there?"

She shook her head.

"I'm guessing you actually have a really good reason for your decision. Not just because it's where the stagecoach goes."

She looked away. "You're a wise man."

"Of course I am. I'm a Texas Ranger." I took a sip of water. Realized I wanted her to look at me again.

"I don't think that has anything to do with you being wise."

"You're pretty wise yourself," I said, nodding slowly.

She smiled again and looked at me. A bevy of butterflies let loose in my stomach.

This girl had me thinking things that I had never thought about.

When I looked into her eyes, I saw a different path from the one I had been on all my life.

And as much as it surprised me that she had my thoughts turned upside down like that, I didn't mind.

The only thing that bothered me was figuring out whether or not I could make that future happen. Turn it from vision to reality.

The thing that made it most unlikely was that it wasn't just my decision to make.

It all hinged on Grace.

Without her the whole thing vanished.

Fifteen

GRACE

Minutes later, the wooden dining room table that had seemed so big and spacious, suddenly seemed much too small.

The stagecoach brought in a whole family. Parents and two children, rowdy from being cooped up all day.

I didn't see a nanny or anyone else to help with the children. The mother, understandably so, looked quite exhausted.

"Do you want to go outside?" Lucas asked. "Go sit out on the porch?"

"Yes," I said, not really wanting to be around anything involving talking about the stagecoach. They would want to talk about how many people they could carry on it and I wasn't ready to hear my fate.

We stepped outside into the relative quietness of early afternoon.

The temperature was already warming up. Spring was just a preview of the scalding summer heat coming up sooner rather than later.

That was probably the one thing that bothered me most about Tucson. The heat. I'd had my fill of it in Louisiana. Having grown up in Philadelphia, I missed the temperate climate there. The pleasant summers. I even missed the winters. Curling up in front of a warm fireplace and spending the afternoon reading a book.

Lucas and I sat side by side in two wooden chairs. Not the most comfortable chairs. Now that I was no long a lady's maid, it would have been nice to have access to a porch swing, especially with Lucas to share it with.

I let myself imagine, for a few minutes, how nice it would have been.

"I've been thinking," Lucas said.

Turning, I looked at him. Whenever I looked into his bright blue eyes, I lost control of my thoughts. They, in fact, took a back seat to my emotions.

It was most disconcerting and pleasant at the same time.

"What have you been thinking about?"

"I've been thinking about hanging up my hat."

I tilted my head to the side. He wasn't wearing a hat at the moment.

"It's a metaphor," he said.

"I know it's a metaphor," I said. "I just didn't know if you knew it."

He laughed and leaned back in his chair.

"Oh. I know it."

"So what are the implications of you hanging up your metaphorical hat?"

"I don't quite know yet." He stretched out his long legs. "But I'm thinking Tucson isn't in there anywhere."

"What's wrong with Tucson?"

"The heat," he said. "A person has to like the heat to consider settling there."

"You don't like the heat?" I asked, but my heart was pounding much too fast at his comment about settling down.

"I'd be happier without it in my life."

I nodded. "I feel the same way about the heat." I didn't tell him that I had just been thinking the same thing. "So if you hang up your hat, I take it you won't be hanging it up in Tucson."

"I'd rather not."

"Do you have some other place in mind you'd like?"

"I might."

We sat in silence for a few minutes. Watched Mr. Parker over next to the barn, getting ready to work on a horseshoe.

"Since you brought it up, you want to share it with me?"

"I don't quite have it all figured out yet."

"I see. Sometimes it's okay to talk about things before you have them figured out. Helps with the figuring."

"You're too wise for me," he said, looking away.

"Probably."

We sat in silence, listening to the children running through the house. I'm sure Mrs. Parker was thrilled with having a couple of wild children racing through her house.

Mr. Parker started hammering on the horseshoe, the loud iron against iron echoing from the barn.

I waited. I figured if Lucas talked to me about what he was thinking, it would be a good sign. Maybe a sign that he was thinking about including me in his plans. If he didn't maybe not so much.

I all but held my breath, forcing myself to wait.

"I'm thinking maybe I'd like to head north. To Colorado."

"Colorado sounds nice." I'd read a dime novel set in Colorado.

I'd read a lot of novels, but the author wove enough magic into that one that it stayed with me.

"Any reason you didn't head there?" He asked.

"The rivers."

"The rivers? What about the rivers?"

"Don't want to cross a river in a wagon. Or a horse. This route—this stagecoach—didn't involve driving a wagon. Or riding a horse. Or the hundred other things involved in getting across the endless prairie to Colorado or Oregon. Especially the rivers."

"I can see you've given this a great deal of thought." He sounded slightly amused. I chose to ignore that.

"I have," I said, with genuine seriousness.

"What would it take to change your mind?"

"I'm not changing my mind about driving a wagon across one of those rivers."

He was smiling at me now.

"I'm serious," I added.

"Fair enough. Take driving the wagon across a river out of the equation."

I took a minute to think that through. Was it possible for me to take it out of my equation?

"You can't do it can you?" he asked.

"I can do it. Just give me a minute."

"I can wait," he said.

"Alright," I turned toward him, settling into the conversation. "What are my options? It all depends on my options. And going back east isn't one of them. I'm committed now to going west."

He nodded. "The west is like that. Once you go west, you don't want to go back."

"I wonder why that is," I said, mostly to myself.

"Because it's a world full of possibilities. A world with its own rules. Its own codes. A man... or woman... can start over and be anything they want to be."

Was that why I was drawn to the west? Because it was a new beginning?

"So," I said. "What are my options?"

He had his answer ready. "Once you reach Tucson, you can head north. Go into the mountains."

"Is there a stagecoach?"

"Not really."

"Then that isn't really an option."

"Anyone ever tell you you're difficult?"

"Never," I said, but I was smiling now and my heart was fluttering with the thought of some of those new possibilities he had spoken of.

Sixteen

LUCAS

Grace and I sat on the porch until the two children scampered outside, giggling and chattering.

A boy and girl, about the same age, around six, but the girl was slightly taller.

A harried-looking nanny trailed behind them, racing behind them toward the barn.

I looked at Grace as the nanny caught up with them and took their hands.

"Did you know there was a nanny?"

"No," she said. "Where did she come from?"

"I don't know." And frankly I didn't care. I was doing the math in my head.

The stagecoach had come in with three adults and two children. There would just be room left over for Flora. Just enough room for Flora.

There would not be room for Grace.

"I'm glad they have a nanny," Grace said. "The mother definitely needs help."

"The children do look like a handful."

"Especially with the mother expecting another baby."

I looked sharply over at Grace. "How could you know that?" We had only seen the mother briefly and we had been outside since. Grace couldn't possibly have had time to talk with her.

She was looking toward the barn, but I swear she batted her eyelashes.

"A girl knows these things."

"You only saw her for a few seconds."

"I just know."

"Do you...?" I swallowed. I wanted to ask, but I wasn't sure I wanted to know the answer. "Do you have children?"

"No," she said, shaking her head. "I'm not married."

I had made assumptions about her that I shouldn't have. A young lady traveling alone might or might not be married. Take Flora, for example, she wasn't exactly young, but she was going to meet her husband.

"Are you betrothed?" I asked, suddenly feeling the need to cover all the possibilities.

"No," she said, glancing at me sideways. "Are you?"

"No. The life of a Texas Ranger isn't conducive for married life."

"I would think that it wouldn't really matter."

"Oh? And why wouldn't it matter?"

"When someone decides to get married, it... it doesn't seem to matter what obstacles they have. They always find a way around them."

I nodded slowly. She was right, of course.

I could blame my lack of a wife on my lifestyle all day long, but the truth was, I had not met a young lady who tempted me to marry.

Until now.

"Are you saying you've never met someone you would marry?"

She answered slowly, as though considering her words carefully "I'm saying that when both people want to marry each other, they always find a way."

I smiled. She was such a romantic and I don't think she even realized it.

"I think you might be right, Miss Grace LaCroix."

"Of course I'm right," she said, smiling at me now. "I've seen it happen."

"Now you have to tell me details," I said.

She rolled her eyes. "And they say men don't gossip."

"Of course we do," I said. "How do you think we know so much?"

Seventeen

GRACE

I didn't tell Lucas about the Amirault family I had worked for. I had specifically been thinking about my friend and employer Daphne.

I had been trying to figure out what if anything to tell Lucas. I wasn't ready to tell anyone about my past.

If I told him about my past, that I had worked as an indentured servant, would it change his opinion of me? Well, technically, I had not been indentured. My mother had. No one asked me to fulfill the terms of her servitude. I had just sort of slid into her place. I'd been given a place to live, food to eat, and all my needs had been taken care of.

I had not been paid money for my services. And it was clear that I was not a guest. I'd had my own private room, but it been a little room on the third floor next to the other servants. There had been a thick braided cord that ran from Daphne's room straight up to mine, a bell on my end. When Daphne pulled the bell cord in her room, I knew she needed me to help her get dressed or do her hair or what-ever else she might need help with at the moment.

Did that make me an indentured servant? It seemed like semantics to me.

Either way, I wasn't ready to share my past with Lucas.

I was saved from having to answer when Flora burst out the front door.

I immediately saw that Flora was trying not to smile. And she wasn't doing such a good job of it in my opinion.

"The stagecoach is leaving in the morning," she said, her hands fisted at her sides.

"I expected as much."

"They don't have room for both of us," she said, then quickly added. "One of us will have to wait for the next stagecoach."

"It's okay, Flora," I said. "I'll wait for the next one."

Flora came right over and hugged me. "You are a dear." Flora turned to Lucas. "She is a dear."

Before either one of us could respond, Flora, practically bursting with excitement, had turned and was on her way back inside.

Lucas turned to me. "You are a dear," he said.

I rolled my eyes.

"Only because I gave up my seat."

"Sort of the definition," he said, taking a cigar out of his coat pocket and sniffing it.

I couldn't help thinking there was more to this man than met the eye. I knew a good quality cigar when I smelled it, and Lucas had a good quality cigar in his hands.

I was, without a doubt, attracted to him, but he had a quality about him that spoke of good breeding and education.

"I guess I'll be staying here a bit longer," I said.

"You have options," he said.

"Options?" I lost my train of thought for a minute as I remembered saying those very same words to Daphne before her arranged marriage. I think I had said something to the effect of there always being options. I told her she could go east or west. And wherever she went, I would go with her.

"Yes," Lucas said. "There are always other options."

"I know, but..." I waved a hand in a vague direction. "Options seem a little limited at the moment."

"Maybe," he said. "Or... you could come with me."

First of all, I was having serious déjà vu. This sounded so much like that conversation I'd had with Daphne, except that I had been on the other side. I had been the one trying to convince her that she had options and I had been the one offering to go with her.

"I don't understand this option," I said, shaking my head. "I don't see any other stagecoaches or trains or well, anything."

"You see horses," he said.

"Horses."

"Those big animals behind the barn." He nodded in that general direction.

I followed his gaze to the horses standing behind the barn.

"No," I said. "You are not getting me on the back of a horse."

Eighteen

LUCAS

"Wait a minute," I said. "Didn't you ride back here with Peter? On the back of his horse?"

"Yes," I said, primly. "but Peter was holding the reins."

I looked at her. Grace was a beautiful young lady. Maybe nineteen at most.

Her hair was dark, framing a perfect heart shaped face. Her bow-shaped lips seemed to be smiling even when she was frowning. Smiling seemed to come much more natural to her than frowning. It was unusual for a woman out here to have smooth features, unmarred by frown lines mostly at their brow. This was the land of furrowed brows.

She was new to the west, I reminded myself. She had yet to endure the hardships that came with life on the frontier.

Life out here was hard, especially on the women. They weren't built for it.

Since Grace was determined to go west, perhaps I could shelter her from those hardships.

I could if she would let me.

I hadn't really thought it through when I'd asked her to come with me.

But now that I'd vocalized it, it began to take on a life of its own.

It was the best idea I had ever had.

Grace and I could go west. We could travel on horseback. No wagon. Or we could get a wagon if we needed to. I'd have to think about that. I'd never traveled across the country with a female.

We could go west a bit, then head north up to Colorado.

There was a town up there. Whiskey Springs. I'd never been there before, but I'd been assured on more than occasion by more than one person that it was the perfect place to settle. It was deep in the Rocky Mountains.

A new town. A fresh start from whatever she was running from.

A young lady didn't just set out on her own traveling west. Not alone and not with no family to go toward.

Not unless the young lady was running away from something. I'd seen that happen on more than one occasion.

She could tell me later whatever it was. If she wanted to. She didn't have to tell me if she didn't want to. It would not change a thing about how I felt about her.

All I had to do was to convince her to come with me. I'd marry her as soon as we ran across a preacher.

But I was getting ahead of myself. Definitely getting ahead of her.

We had to move one step at the time.

The first thing I had to do was to get her on a horse.

Even if we decided to purchase a wagon, we'd have to do it later on. There wasn't anything here to even think about buying. This was a stagecoach route. Not a pioneer-wagon route.

"Come on." I stood up and held out a hand.

"Come on where?" she asked, looking at me sideways.

"You're about to have your first riding lesson."

"Nah uh" she said. "Not getting on a horse. Only if someone I trust is holding the reins."

"You can trust me."

"I don't think so."

"But you trusted Peter."

"Peter was holding the reins."

"I'll hold the reins."

"No," she said, looking up at me. "You want me to ride by myself."

"I—"

"No. I'm not doing it."

Nineteen

GRACE

Half an hour later I sat on the back of an old mare named Star as Lucas and I made our way along the main road leading west.

Lucas walked, holding Star's reins. It was part of the deal. The whole deal as far as I was concerned.

"I don't think she can go very far," I said. I sat astride, my green skirts belled out around me flowing on either side of the horse. Needless to say, I did not own a riding habit and even if I did, it would be in my trunks in Miller's Creek.

"It's okay," he said. "That's the whole point of you being on her and not a horse like mine." I'd met his horse, a spirited stallion he called Sparky who shifted his paws and snorted as we walked past his stall.

"I knew it was a trick," I said.

Lucas grinned. "Old Star here wouldn't go anywhere even if I dropped the reins."

A shot of panic shot through my system. "Let's not test that out."

"No," Lucas said. "I told you. You can trust me."

I nodded. "It's okay. I can do this." I refused to be afraid.

"Let's just ride around a bit. Get you used to sitting on her back."

"You might recall, I rode several miles yesterday," I said.

"Right," he said, face brightening. "You did, didn't you? We can move the lessons up a notch."

"Or we can just walk around a bit. Make sure she's used to me."

"She doesn't seem concerned."

"This isn't all about her," I said, then smiled to offset my testy tone.

"You're right," he said. "It's about the two of you."

I rolled my eyes Heavenward. "Um. Lucas?"

"You're doing fine." He reached over and patted Old Star's nose.

"No," I said. "It's not that."

Something in my voice caught his attention.

"What's wrong?"

"There," I said. "I think there's a storm coming this way."

He followed my gaze. "I think you're right."

We were a little ways away from the inn now. probably half a mile or so at least.

And we had somehow ridden right toward the very nasty, very dark roiling dark clouds without realizing it.

I looked back over my shoulder. "It was so clear. It's still clear back behind us."

"That's how it works out here."

"What do we do?"

"We go back to the inn," he said.

Lightning flashed in the dark rolling clouds ahead followed shortly by a loud clap of thunder.

"We need to go now," I said, suddenly wishing I did know how to ride a horse. I could turn her around and gallop back to the inn. I couldn't, of course, leave Lucas out here in the storm.

The storm was moving quickly, already tugging my hair loose from my bonnet and tossing strands of it into my face.

Lucas handed me the reins.

"Oh no," I said.

"Just for a minute."

I held onto the reins, fully expecting Old Star to bolt at any minute. She would bolt, running blindly. Frightened by the storm.

We would be lost. And no one would ever find us.

I struggled to take a breath. I felt dizzy and I might have fainted if I had been standing. My eyes blurred and I couldn't focus.

Before I knew what he was doing, Lucas had mounted the horse behind me.

He took the reins from my hands and turned Old Star around.

"Are you okay?" he asked.

Considering that I couldn't catch my breath, no.

I couldn't speak.

I shook my head.

Thunder continued to crash behind us, but we were moving away from it.

It wouldn't catch us.

With Old Star moving steadily beneath us, we continued to move slowly but surely in the direction of the inn.

"Grace," Lucas said, his breath against my ear.

I didn't answer.

"Grace." He wrapped his arms around me and pressed me back against him. "Close your eyes. Breathe with me."

It took a minute, but I did. I relaxed against him and breathed with him. In and out. In and out.

I breathed with him until I was breathing steady again.

I realized we had stopped and the wind was no longer whipping around us.

Opening my eyes, I saw that we were back inside the barn.

"Better?" he asked.

"Yes," I said on a breath.

"You're okay. You're safe."

I closed my eyes again.

"What happened?"

"You lost your breath," he said. "But you're okay now."

"Yes," I said. "I'm okay."

But maybe I wasn't. I now knew why I was afraid of horses and I knew what had really happened to my father.

Twenty

LUCAS

I held Grace tightly against me. It was all I knew to do and I did that by instinct.

She had been in distress.

I'd seen it before with soldiers coming off the battlefield.

It was funny. After battle, they didn't usually start reacting right away. Sometimes it took days or even weeks. Usually the first sign was having nightmares. Or they froze the next time they found themselves on the battlefield or even in a dangerous situation.

But this thing with Grace... I had never seen a woman with battle distress.

Something must have happened to her. Whether it was the horse or the storm or both, I couldn't fathom.

We sat there, my arms wrapped around her, holding her tightly, the pungent smell of hay mixed with the scent of rain splashing against the dry ground.

I knew the moment she began to calm. I could feel it in her breathing.

"Better?" I asked softly, my cheek pressed against the back of her head. Her hair smelled like jasmine.

She nodded. "Yes." I barely heard her answer, even being this close.

"Let's get you down," I said. "Get you some water to drink."

"Okay." She was trembling.

I dismounted and turned and put my hands on her waist to help her from the horse. She put her hands on my shoulders, her fingers digging into my skin.

With her feet on the ground, I didn't release her right away. Instead, I slid my hands up, keeping them on her elbows, making sure she was steady on her feet.

"I'm okay," she said, trying a wobbly smile.

"Come sit over here," I said, leading her over to a barrel.

It was a tall barrel. Too tall for her to sit on without assistance. So I put my hands on her waist again and lifted her up, depositing her on the top of the barrel.

"You'll be okay here for a minute?" I asked.

She nodded. Then put a hand on my arm. "You'll get wet."

Thunder rumbled overhead as though to punctuate her words.

"It's okay," I said. "I promise. I'll be right back."

With one last glance in her direction, I headed out to the well.

Rain pummeled over my head as I wound the lever to pull the heavy pail up from the bottom of the well.

My protective instincts were on high alert.

I hated leaving her alone even just long enough to go out to the well for water.

I was worried about her and I wanted to protect her.

The feeling was not new to me, at least not exactly.

As a Texas Ranger, it was my job to protect people every day.

But this was different. This was more intense. More personal.

Not only did I want to protect her, I wanted to hold her close to me. She was fragile and vulnerable and yet strong all at the same time.

I took the pail with me and went back to the barn. The storm had moved out, leaving nothing more than a few lingering raindrops.

The storm had moved out as quickly as it had appeared. The sun, even, was out again.

I was soaked all the way to the skin now, my pants making a squishing sound when I walked. Needed to get to the inn. Put on some dry clothes. Fortunately we had reached the barn before Grace had gotten wet.

Once inside the shadowed barn, I gave myself a moment for my eyes to adjust. I took a step toward the barrel where I had left Grace.

I froze.

Grace was gone.

Twenty-One

GRACE

After Lucas stepped out into the pouring rain, I sat there for all of about two minutes before I slid off the barrel.

The storm was moving out already. Nothing more than a wave of havoc passing through, leaving mud puddles everywhere. They wouldn't be there long. The sun would soak them right up, leaving the ground dry and cracked again.

Using the pale light shining in from the open barn door, I went to Sparky's stall. Lucas's horse was big. Majestic.

My hands trembling and hesitant, I placed my palm on the side of his neck. He didn't pull away. He leaned in, looking at me with his big brown eyes.

"You're beautiful, aren't you? And loyal."

He didn't answer, of course.

I dropped my hand and leaned against the stall door, studying him.

But it wasn't Sparky that I was really seeing.

I was seeing something else.

As we had ridden back to the barn, a memory had returned to me in full force.

Contrary to what I remembered, I had not been sitting at my desk translating Latin when my father had been run down by a carriage.

He had, in fact, not been run down by a carriage at all.

I had been with him. I'd been with Father that day. I had been sitting in front of him much as I had ridden with Lucas.

My father had loved to ride. Horses were his passion. A business man by trade, he actually made his money in horse trading.

Most Saturdays when the weather was nice, we would get up early in the morning before dawn and ride to the park on the edge of town.

That day my father had let me take the reins of the horse.

I remembered it now.

It had been early. A morning following a rain storm and mist hovered over the ground. Probably not the best time to be out riding.

Sitting on the back of his stallion, we had raced across an open field.

After that I only remembered bits and pieces. Jumbled little snippets of memories like scrambled pieces of a jigsaw puzzle. Each individual snippet meant nothing, but when I put them together, they gave me a memory. Not a well formed memory, necessarily, but a vague memory.

I remembered a white picket fence looming ahead. I think Father grabbed the reins, but I couldn't know. At the last minute, with the mist hovering above the ground, distorting the horse's perception, the horse came to an abrupt and sudden unexpected stop.

Both my father and I had been thrown from the horse.

I had lost consciousness and must have had a concussion. My

next memory was me lying in my bed, my mother looking at me with sad eyes and feeding me chicken soup.

Somehow during that time, my mother had invented a kinder story for me. The version where I had been home when my father had lost his life.

That version my mother had invented for me had served me well for over ten years.

I'd never known why I didn't want to ride on the back of a horse. I'd ride in a carriage or a wagon. I had even ridden when Peter had been holding the reins.

But when the storm approached us and Lucas had handed me Old Star's reins, something had broken loose in my mind, letting that horrible memory out.

I preferred to push it back down where it belonged. Out of my head. So far down I could never reach it again.

But I didn't know if that was possible. I had traveled west and as much as I might want it to be different, I had come out here where the main mode of transportation was riding on the back of a horse.

If I was going to survive, I was going to have to learn how to ride a horse. Actually... I knew how to ride a horse.

I was going to have to learn how to tolerate riding on the back of a horse. Holding the reins myself.

Lucas was the one who could do that for me. Lucas could get me past my terror of being on the back of a horse if anyone could.

At least now I understood where that fear came from.

Understanding where it came from meant I could fight it.

Maybe, just maybe, I could get past it enough to travel to Colorado with Lucas.

I had started this journey with no more than a destination in mind. A place I knew nothing about and knew no one there.

It would be much better to travel to a place where I knew nothing about, but where Lucas would be.

Turning around, I saw him standing there with a pail of water in one hand, looking at me.

"I brought you some water," he said, lifting the pail.

Lucas had brought me more than water.

Lucas had brought me hope.

Twenty-Two

LUCAS

As I stood watching Grace, I again wondered what she was thinking.

She was watching Sparky, thinking her mysterious thoughts—mysterious to me anyway.

I had grown up with a father left to raise three kids after his wife died in childbirth with his third. I had been seven at the time.

There had been nothing I could do. Not one single damn thing.

The memory of that helpless feeling still haunted me at times.

After that happened, I had challenged that need to protect into something good—becoming a Texas Ranger.

Maybe I had been running from having a family.

But right now, gazing at Grace, I recognized the empty spot that Grace so easily slid into.

She was right for me. perfect even.

I could help her get past whatever demons haunted her. I was certain of it.

I could get her past them or die trying.

Dipping the gourd tied by a piece of rope into the water bucket, I handed her a drink of water.

As she drank, she kept her gaze locked on mine.

"Thank you," she said, handing me the empty gourd.

"You're welcome," I said.

"You should get into some dry clothes," she said.

"I will," I said, taking a drink myself. "How are you?"

"Better," she said.

I recognized the forced smile on her lips and the haunted look in her eyes. She wasn't as well as she wanted me to think. Grace was tough. She was going to do well as a frontierswoman whether she knew it or not.

"Lucas," she said. "I've had some things happen in my past. Bad things."

"You can tell me if you want to, but you don't have to. You don't have to explain anything to me."

We walked together out of the barn and started across the street.

"A lot of people come out here because they had bad things happen to them."

"How do we get past it? How do we let those things go?" she asked, looking into my eyes, searching for answers I didn't have.

"Some people don't. Some people are haunted by those things their entire lives."

"What about the others? How do they get past those things?"

"Life is lived forward, Ma chérie," I said. "All we have is right now. We have to point ourselves toward the future and live each day to the fullest."

She took a deep breath and nodded as we walked up the stairs to the front door.

"Has anyone ever told you that you are a wise man?" she asked before we went inside.

"Actually yes. I was told that once by a very wise woman."

I took her hand and kissed the back of her fingertips.

She wasn't trembling anymore and her smile was more relaxed.

Yes. I could help her get past her demons. And she could help me get past mine.

Mrs. Parker, holding a broom in one hand, opened the front door.

"Oh dear," she said, taking one look at me. "You got caught out in the storm. Get in here and get yourself into some dry clothes. You do have dry clothes, don't you?"

"Yes ma'am," I said, looking over at Grace. "I'll see you in a few minutes."

"Oh, Captain Roberts," Mrs. Parker said. "A letter came for you."

"A letter? I didn't see a rider."

"You were in the barn, I think." She swept a little pile of dirt out the door and kept talking. "He didn't so much as get off his horse. Wouldn't even take anything to eat. The young man was in quite a hurry."

Twenty-Three

GRACE

I sat alone at the big wooden table for eight and sipped hot tea from a warm mug.

After Lucas broke the seal and quickly read the letter that had come for him, he went to his room and took the letter with him.

Whatever it was, it was bad news. I saw it on his face.

I didn't know if it was work or personal, but I was inclined to think it was personal. He didn't say anything, but his expression was that of a wounded man.

I felt bad for him. Wanted to soothe his pain. But it was hardly my place.

Flora was in the kitchen with Mrs. Parker, the two of them appeared to have become fast friends. It was unfortunate that Flora had to leave on the stagecoach first thing in the morning.

I was quickly learning that the west could be a lonely place. A place where people rarely stayed in the same place for very long. Most people who had the temperament to come out west had the accompanying temperament to chase the next opportunity.

They had pulled up their roots, shaken the dirt off, and given up any semblance of stability.

It made sense to me that once a person had done that, made that first move, the next move was easier. Moving, in fact, became a way of life. Expected, even.

I felt that way myself. My roots had been pulled up when I was sixteen. When my mother had ran away from her old life into a new uncertain life.

That was what made it so easy for me to leave with Daphne last year. I couldn't help wondering what Daphne must have gone through as she made the decision to move to Boston with her husband. She must have been terrified. Daphne had lived her entire life in the same place. She hadn't even gone off to finishing school like her sister Jade.

I looked forward to finding a place to settle again. I had enjoyed my time with the Amiraults, but I had been a worker. I wanted a home of my own where I was the lady of the house.

Moving out west seemed to be the best way to make that possible. I would get my own home and take in sewing or maybe even tutoring. Surely there would be children who needed to learn French. I might even brush up on my Latin and offer to tutor someone in that, too. Someone, like me, who was thirsty for knowledge.

As I finished my tea, Lucas came to the door. He carried another mug and a teapot.

"There you are," he said. He had changed into dry clothes that looked almost exactly like the clothes he changed out of.

"Mrs. Parker sent this along," he said, pulling out a chair next to mine and sitting down.

Him sitting next to me like this never got old and I was fairly certain it never would.

"Tea?" he asked, sliding my mug over for a refill when I nodded.

"Are you okay?" I asked.

Grimacing, he sat back in the chair and stared into his mug. "I will be."

"Anything you want to talk about?"

He hesitated, not answering right away.

I knew how to be patient. To wait until a person was ready to talk. Learned from those years of being a lady's maid.

"It's one of those things I can't do anything about," he said. "Just turn toward the future and keep moving, right?"

"Right," I said.

Easier said than done and we both knew it.

Twenty-Four

LUCAS

The next morning dawned bright and sunny. A perfect day for travel. Any signs of yesterday's storm were gone. The ground was back to its dry, dusty state.

A big solid black lab chased at the chickens, not to catch them, but to watch them fly.

"Biscuit," Mr. Parker called from the barn door. "Cut it out."

Biscuit turned and wagged his tail, then he took off racing about a hundred yards to the west, then turned and raced back to the barn, skidding to a halt at Mr. Parker's feet.

The two of them went inside the barn, Mr. Parker keeping up a steady conversation with the dog.

The Parkers were good people. I couldn't understand why they had chosen to settle here. It wasn't a place I would have picked to live.

Maybe they had made it this far, then decided they'd had enough of traveling. It was hard to say. Personally, I wanted to live someplace where the weather wasn't hot. I'd had my share of cold weather, but I'd choose it any day over this heat.

And now I had no reason to return to Virginia. There was nothing left there for me.

It saddened me, but I also found it freeing. Somewhere in the back of my mind there had always lingered a nagging thought that I should visit my father one more time.

Now that opportunity had passed.

All in all, I wasn't sure how I was supposed to feel. So I chose not to think about it at all.

After Grace and I watched Flora and the little family including the harried nanny, board the stagecoach and roll away, we came to a truce.

The Parkers, understandably, didn't want to sell their horse, Old Star, so we agreed that Grace would ride on the horse with me until we found a suitable horse for her.

I was still thinking about the wagon. Thinking hard about it. We had a long route ahead of us and we could carry a lot of supplies in one. It didn't seem right taking a woman on a trek like this without one. There might be inns all along the way to Tucson, but once we headed north toward Colorado, that would change.

I could not have Grace sleeping on the ground.

"Have you ever driven a wagon?" I asked.

My question seemed to startle her out of wherever her thoughts had taken her.

"As in actually drive?"

"Yes. Drive." I already knew the answer. If it involved holding the reins of a horse, then Grace avoided it.

"No," she said, shaking her head. I was always a passenger."

"Hmm." A passenger. That could only mean one thing. Grace

was from a wealthy family. If she had never driven a wagon and always had a coachman, then it was the most reasonable explanation.

"What?" she said, looking over her shoulder.

When she turned, she couldn't have known that I had my head bent forward near hers.

She was so close now that I could feel the breath coming from her parted lips.

Her gaze dipped to my mouth and that was it. There was no way I was going to let this moment pass without kissing her.

It only required the smallest of movements and it helped that Sparky shifted to avoid one of those potholes.

My lips pressed against hers for a kiss that was sweeter than honey.

If I'd had any lingering doubt about being smitten by Grace, that lingering doubt was gone. Just vanished.

With this simple kiss, I knew that she was the one. The one I wanted to wake up next to for the rest of my life.

Twenty-Five

GRACE

By the time we reached Miller's Creek, my life had changed.

Lucas had kissed me.

I leaned back against him, his strong arms keeping me firmly on the horse, and replayed that simple kiss over and over.

I could still feel his lips on mine. Soft and firm at the same time. I still had tingles shooting through my blood, my heart raced. It was especially so since I sitting with my back pressed up against him. That did not help.

My first kiss. Could he tell it was my first kiss?

A kiss changed everything for a lady.

A kiss usually meant marriage.

Lucas had said nothing about marriage.

We passed a little farmhouse, then another, a sure sign that we were quickly approaching Miller's Creek.

Something was bothering me and I couldn't quite figure out what it was.

"We'll stop here for dinner," Lucas said. "In Miller's Creek."

"Didn't Mrs. Parker send fried chicken and mashed potatoes?"

"She did. It's hard to forget with it smelling like it does."

"It smells good to me," I said.

"She's a good woman," Lucas said. "Sure and steady. But I can't help but wonder why they settled there."

"I know why," I said.

"Do you now? Well, you have to tell me."

"There you go with the gossip thing again."

"Men don't call it gossip. We call it gathering information."

I rolled my eyes, but he could have asked me just about anything right now and I would answer him.

"They had been traveling in a stagecoach together. They didn't know each other before that. When they stopped back there at Horsehead, there was nothing there. No house or anything. While they were taking a break to stretch their legs, the stagecoach was robbed and they were left with nothing."

"What kind of story is this?" he asked.

I laughed. "I thought you wanted the true story."

"Since it obviously has a happy ending, you can go ahead."

"Gee. Thanks. Anyway, while they were camped there, trying to figure out what to do next, Mr. Parker proposed to Mrs. Parker. So the place has a lot of meaning for them. They decided to stay. Right there. They built their house and added a barn soon after."

"That's a romantic story," he said. "What do you think about all that?"

"I don't think it's very practical and I don't see why anyone would want to live out here."

"That's a relief," he said.

"Why is that?" I asked as the inn, a two-story whitewashed house that looked completely out of place out here in the barren land, came into view.

"It means you won't be asking me to go back and build a house on that spot where I kissed you."

"That's different," I said, mostly to myself.

It might be different, technically, but for me it was life-altering. I saw the world differently now. I wasn't even minding the hot wind blowing dirt into my hair.

"We're here," he said stopping and securing Sparky's reins on a hitching post.

As he helped me down from the horse's back, I realized what was bothering me.

Lucas didn't know anything about my past. He didn't know that I had gone from being a wealthy businessman's daughter to being destitute and working as a lady's maid.

Was a lady's maid still considered a lady?

It seemed quite likely, but no one had ever confirmed that for me.

Well, I wasn't a lady's maid anymore. I was back to being the Grace who had left her home in Philadelphia. Maybe I could just forget about those years in between.

But then I would be forgetting about Daphne and Jade and the rest of the Amirault and Beausejour families next door.

That wasn't an option for me.

I just had to make sure Lucas didn't find out about my past. About my time as a lady's maid or, maybe especially, the year I had spent working as a waitress.

It was important that he continue to see me as a lady.

Twenty-Six

LUCAS

After getting Grace settled in the inn's dining room, I took care of Sparky. Got him settled into a stall for the night.

Grace was always relatively quiet, but she seemed even more quiet, it seemed, as we neared Miller's Creek.

I chalked it up to the stress of riding with a strange man. Alone.

Where she was from, and technically me, too, a lady didn't go on long unchaperoned rides with a male who wasn't a close relative.

She was taking quite the risk.

I liked that about her.

Although she might be afraid of taking the reins of a horse, she was fearless in every other way I had seen so far.

I was a lucky man to have found her.

"I'll be right back," I'd told her. "I have to take care of a small matter."

"Or course. Take your time," she said. "I'll be here. Trying to find my trunk."

Right. Her clothes and other personal items were supposed to be here waiting for her.

She would be wanting a bath.

I ran across the proprietor and asked if she would please see to it that Grace got a hot bath and soon.

Assured that it would happen, I crossed the street to the General Store.

"I need to send a letter," I said.

"Sure thing," the man behind the counter said. "For two bits more, you can make it a telegraph."

"Okay. Telegraph then."

I nodded and picked up a pencil. I didn't say anything.

"Ready when you are," he said.

It would have been so much easier to just write a letter. A man could ramble around in a letter and say what he wanted to say in his own good time.

But a telegraph. That required a little more thought. I had to reduce my thoughts down to ten words or less.

Maybe that was better anyway. Maybe it was better to just get to the point.

"I'll come back," I said.

"Take your time," the man said as I headed out the door.

Thinking about the telegraph, I walked across the street and found a nice prairie schooner wagon that the owner was willing to part with for a fair price. Bought from another couple, mid-aged now who had decided to stop and settle right here.

The guy who sold me the wagon knew a guy with some horses he might be willing to sell, so within a short amount of time I had myself a wagon and two horses to pull it.

By the time all my business was taken care of, I had decided what I wanted to say in my telegraph.

The man behind the counter took down my words without so much as blinking an eye. He had no doubt heard just about everything.

With all my business out of the way, I could go and break the news to Grace that we were now the owners of an outfitted prairie schooner.

She wouldn't even have to drive it. I could do that. Sparky could follow along behind us.

I was frankly looking forward to having that time alone with her. I wanted to know everything about her.

I would, of course, still be sleeping on the ground, but Grace would not and that was all that mattered.

Twenty-Seven

GRACE

I paced the dining room while I waited for Lucas to return, stopping to look out the window at every turn. I didn't even try to pretend that I wasn't waiting for him.

This inn, a house really, was run by a woman. No husband. The only men were the men who worked for her.

She'd had them draw me up a hot bath in no time. Now that I had my trunk, I picked out a fresh dress and put it on after my bath.

It was wonderful to feel civilized again.

According to Lucas, once we headed north to Colorado, inns would be few and far between. Nonexistent, really.

I wasn't sure about the whole sleeping on the ground part, though it wasn't the ground itself. It was what crawled around on the ground. I'd lived in the south long enough to be quite familiar with snakes.

I'd rather face a rabid wolf any day over a snake. A rabid wolf would announce itself in time to shoot it. A snake on the other hand was sly and sneaky. Hiding out, just waiting for the right time to strike.

I paced to the door and back to the window.

This time I was rewarded. Lucas was coming this way.

I quickly went to the parlor and sat down on the sofa. There was no reason to let him know that I had been waiting for him.

I arranged my pretty green skirts around me with dots of pink flowers and managed to look quite relaxed by the time the door opened and Lucas walked in.

"Grace?" he called.

"I'm in the parlor."

He was smiling. His business must have gone well.

He sat down in an armchair across from me.

"I have good news," he said.

"You found us a stagecoach." It wasn't that I minded riding on Sparky with him, it was what would happen when he decided it was time for me to ride my own horse.

We weren't far from that. I was certain of it.

"No." He looked a bit concerned. "We decided to travel on our own, right? To go north to Colorado."

"That's right," I said, looking up at him with a little smile. "I remember now."

"Uh huh. Well. I bought us a wagon and two horses to pull it."

I gaped at him. "How?"

"Well. I found people willing to sell."

"So fast," I said, realizing that my whole adult life, I'd had to scrimp and think about things before I bought them. I had forgotten what it was like to not have to worry about every penny. To calculate how much money I had before I bought something.

It looked like we were going to be staying here for the night. It didn't seem to concern him that we hadn't made it very far today. Perhaps we'd make better time with a wagon.

"I couldn't let you sleep on the ground."

I nodded. Having never been in a wagon, much less slept in one, I didn't know how it worked.

My mother had planned our trip well enough that we had traveled to the south mostly by train. It was a long time ago, but it hadn't been bad.

"Does that mean you'll be sleeping on the ground?"

"Unless you're going to marry me, I guess it does."

Twenty-Eight

LUCAS

The inn here in Miller's Creek wasn't as nice as the one in Horsehead, but it was clean and had a cozy feel to it.

A fire burned low in the fireplace, warding off the chill coming on the heels of the setting sun.

The proprietor, a woman's name I could not recall at the moment, quietly took care of business, leaving us alone.

Grace hid her emotions well, but I saw the surprise when it flashed across her features for just a moment when I mentioned the word marriage.

"Well, I guess you'll be sleeping on the ground then," she said.

"I've done it before."

"You're going to get cold. Did you buy blankets?"

"Not yet. We'll go to the General Store first thing in the morning and get whatever we'll need for the trip."

"Okay," she said with some uncertainty.

"Maybe you should get some sleep," I said. "It's been a long day."

"Our long days are just getting started, aren't they?"

"I'd say that's a fair assumption."

"Don't people make these trips in groups?"

"Usually."

"But we're going alone."

"Unless we happen across a group."

"That doesn't worry you? To be out there alone?"

"I prefer it, actually," I said. "Anytime a group of people travel like that, close together, things have a tendency to turn to trouble."

"Seems like it would be safer," she said.

"If it would make you feel better, I can ask around. See if there are any wagon trains heading in our direction."

"Okay," she said. What if something happened to Lucas out there? I'd be all alone. "I think that might be a good idea. Just in case something happens."

"We'll check at the General Store in the morning. See if there are any ads."

"Good," she said, looking at me from beneath her lashes. She looked a little confused.

"What's troubling you?" I asked.

"Nothing. I was just thinking about what would happen once we get there. To Colorado. I don't know anything about the country."

"You didn't know anything about Tucson either, right?"

"No... but I had talked to a lot of people. Got their recommendations."

I grinned. "I don't think you talked to the right people, Grace."

"Maybe." She looked away.

Outside the front of the house someone rode past on a horse and two young boys shouted at each other as they raced along the street heading in the opposite direction.

"Grace," I said. "I can make you a promise."

She lifted her gaze to mine and I looked into those mesmerizing green eyes of hers. Eyes I wanted to just fall into and never come out.

"What promise?"

"I promise that as long as I have breath, I will make sure you're taken care of."

"You don't have to—"

"I know I don't," I said. "But I've made my decision. It's time for me to leave the Texas Rangers and find a new place in the world."

"Will they really let you do that? Just leave the state?"

"They'll be okay." And I knew they would. Either way, I would be better off with Grace. It was time for me to settle down.

Twenty-Nine

GRACE

After digging through my trunk and finding a nightgown, I crawled into the little bed I'd been provided.

It was a small bed and not nearly so nice as the one at Horsehead Crossing. On the positive side, I wasn't having to share a bed. Being alone made up for the meager furnishings.

The linens smelled fresh, so that was a plus as well.

I wondered where Flora and the little family had stopped for the night. They would have stopped here briefly, then gone on their way.

Then my thoughts made their way back to Lucas.

I replayed his kiss in my head, then mentally went over our conversation.

He had promised he would take care of me. As long as he had breath.

That was a serious statement. One a man shouldn't make lightly.

It was hard for me to gauge Lucas's intentions.

He threw around the word marriage, but I'd seen no sign of a proposal.

If, and it was a big if, he wanted to marry me, there was no one for him to ask for permission. No father to ask for my hand. Not even a brother. Or my mother for that matter.

When I had lived with the Amiraults I had never felt alone. I had always felt like a part of the family.

Now that I had left that, willingly, things were different.

I truly was alone. The only person I had was Lucas. What if he changed his mind?

It terrified me to think about what I would do if he changed his mind about taking care of me, especially out in the middle of nowhere. I didn't have any reason to think that he would, but I was going on blind faith.

I could take care of myself. That wasn't the problem. My self-sufficiency went as far as the city limits. It was going out in the middle of nowhere that bothered me.

It was hard to think straight. My thoughts were clouded by that one kiss.

If I'd known that it would have such a profound effect on me, I might would have found someone a long time ago to kiss. I'd certainly had lots of opportunities.

But they would not have been Lucas. The whole experience would have been completely different.

I could tell him no. I could wait here at Miller's Creek and take the next coach maybe even as soon as tomorrow.

But Lucas had been so proud that he had bought a wagon and two horses. He planned on us buying supplies in the morning.

I didn't know what kind of supplies a person would need out on the trail, but I was certain he did.

I couldn't do it. I couldn't tell him no.

If he was anyone else, I probably would have. I'd have continued on my planned path to Tucson. But Lucas had gotten into my heart.

I thought about him every minute. All I wanted to do was to be near him.

He had joked about getting married so he wouldn't have to sleep on the ground.

My mother used to tell me there's always a grain of truth in a joke. I'd always believed that to be true.

If that was true, then maybe there was a possibility that Lucas wanted to marry me.

Between my mother's teachings and the lessons of propriety I had learned from watching Daphne grow into an adult, I knew how a lady behaved.

I also knew that what men wanted most was that thing they couldn't have.

I would have to tread lightly. To protect my heart.

And knowing that hurt my heart more than anything.

Thirty

LUCAS

Sitting in a chair out in back of the house, I watched the full moon rise above the trees and smoked a cigar. I didn't normally smoke cigars, but the owner of the General Store had given it to and it just seemed wrong to let it go to waste.

I felt good. Damn good.

I had made one of those life changing decision that a man doubted until he did it, then he knew he was doing the right thing.

That's how I felt about Grace.

I had her going to Colorado with me. Something that was still hard to believe.

But I wanted more. I wanted to marry her.

I wanted her to be my wife and I didn't want to wait until we got to Whiskey Springs.

Patience had never been my virtue, but it looked like I was going to have to learn some.

Grace didn't seem to be jumping to marry me.

I couldn't blame her, after all, we had just met.

That was the thing about a man, or so I had heard. I'd always heard that when a man found the woman he wanted to marry, it hit him like a ton of rocks. It had never happened to me, but it couldn't since I only just met Grace.

I blew out a smoke ring. Watched it until blended into the darkness. A dog or maybe a wolf howled in the distance. A few minutes later, another one answered.

I was taking Grace out into the middle of nowhere. I might be a Texas Ranger, but I was just one man.

If there was trouble with Indians or outlaws I could only do so much.

If something happened to me, she would be in danger and wouldn't have anyone to help her.

She was absolutely right. I could not in good conscience take her on the trail to Colorado alone. We needed a group.

We'd head out of here tomorrow, follow along the Goodnight Stagecoach Road until we came to El Paso. Surely we could find some likeminded people there to travel with.

If not, well then, we could stay in El Paso until next year. That would give us more time to plan.

And it would give us time to get married.

Neither one of us would be sleeping on the ground.

With that thought, I put out my cigar and went back inside.

I needed to get some sleep. Tomorrow would be a busy day.

The house was quiet with everyone gone to bed.

The house wasn't as nice as the house in Horsehead, but it had a cozy feeling to it.

I didn't know much, anything really, about the lady who lived here and ran the inn. I assumed she had been married at one time.

Someone who just ended up here.

I would build a nice house for Grace in Whiskey Springs. A nice two-story house with lots of room for children. We would have a big family.

Now all I had to do was to convince her to marry me.

She was here, I reminded myself. And tomorrow we were continuing our journey together. We were going to Colorado Territory. Together. It would be the adventure of a lifetime and that was saying a lot for a Texas Ranger.

I was most definitely ready to start the next chapter of my life.

Thirty-One

GRACE

"What else do you think we need?" Lucas asked.

We stood in the middle of the General Store among barrels of flour, candles, and blankets just to name just a few. The shelves were packed with such a variety of things. There were bolts of cloth stored next to a glass jar of peppermints.

Back in Philadelphia, I would have gone to a different store for every one of those items. Even in Vicksburg where I often went shopping with Daphne had lots of specialty stores. But here one store carried everything.

I looked at the stack of items on the counter. We had blankets, a sack of flour, and some of those candles. Lots of candles. And beans.

"It seems like we're going to need more food," I said. "How can we live off flour and beans?"

"I'll go hunting. We'll have food. But..." He gazed around the store. "Let's get some of those apples and potatoes. Whatever else you can find that we might possibly need."

"Okay."

"I'll be back in a few minutes."

"Where are you going?"

"I'm going to see if I can find us a couple of chickens to take with us. Maybe a cow."

I stared at his back as he went outside to ask about procuring livestock.

What else did we need? Perhaps the real question was what didn't we need?

I added an iron skillet to our stack of things. A couple of plates. A basin. Silverware.

Salt. I looked around the store. We needed salt.

And a barrel for water.

This was a rather frightening task Lucas had left me with. If we forgot one little thing, our whole trip could go wrong.

I went up to the clerk standing behind the counter.

"Can you help me?" I asked.

"Sure thing," he said, lowering his spectacles. "What do you need?"

"I think we need everything."

"Heading west, huh?"

"So it seems."

"Well," he said, coming around the counter. "Looks like you've got a pretty good start here. Maybe some soap. And let's see..."

Within fifteen minutes, we had more than I ever thought I would buy in one place at one time.

I kept my money pinned in the waistband of my skirt, so I needed a moment of privacy to pull it out.

"How much do I owe you?" I asked.

"You don't owe me anything," he said.

"But..." I looked over the pile of things we'd chosen for the trip. We owed something and not a little bit.

"Your husband already paid."

"My—" I clamped my mouth shut.

We might be heading into the wild west, but I could protect my reputation if people thought we were married.

Even if we weren't.

"Is that your wagon out front?" he asked, nodding toward the Conestoga wagon with its white canopy.

"Looks like it," I said. I recognized the two horses Lucas had so proudly introduced me to.

"You wait here," he said. "Help yourself to some water. I'll take this out to your wagon.

"I'm sure Lucas will be back shortly."

"Well then, we'll surprise him, yes?"

"Yes." I smiled and felt some of the tension draining away.

This wasn't going to be so bad. This was going to be an adventure.

I was going to Colorado with Lucas. And if he just happened to want to marry me along the way, so much the better.

If he did marry me, maybe I wouldn't mind.

When I saw Lucas heading back toward the store carrying a crate of chickens, I knew I didn't mind one little bit.

Thirty-Two

LUCAS

I'd traveled all across Texas, often into dangerous territory. But I had never felt the nervousness I was feeling right now.

I couldn't quite put my finger on where the nerves were coming from.

Everything was as it should be.

Grace and I had a wagon full of supplies that hopefully would last us at least until we got to El Paso.

Since it had taken a while to get everything packed in the wagon —whoever said packing a Conestoga wagon was easy didn't know what they were talking about—we decided to stay in Miller's Creek for lunch.

I wanted to make things as easy on Grace as I could even if that meant we took our time getting to our next stop.

After we ate a quick meal, I went out to hook up the horses and double-checked that everything was ready to go.

Grace went back to her room for something. She was rather

vague about what. That didn't concern me. I knew that ladies needed more privacy than men. It was all part of their charm.

Pulling out my pocket watch, I checked the time.

She had been gone a lot longer than I had expected. I knew she wasn't changing clothes because all her things were packed in the wagon.

Finished hooking up the horses, I took a long look around. Everything seemed to be as it should be.

A woman walked into the General Store with a little boy in tow. She was holding tightly to his hand to keep him from running. Somebody had recently fed the chickens. The dozen or so of them were pecking the ground like crazy.

I wasn't seeing any danger.

Why then were the hackles on the back of my neck up?

I could almost feel the tension thrumming through my body.

Maybe it was simply because I hadn't seen Grace in—I checked my watch again—nearly an hour.

She was taking too long.

I slammed my pocket watch closed and stuffed it back into my pocket.

Something was wrong.

Leaving the horses and the wagon and everything right there, unattended, I walked across the dusty road to the inn.

It was quiet inside. The owner, Mrs. Tidwell, was nowhere to be seen. I'd say I finally remembered her name, but it was Grace who talked to her. Grace who had gotten the woman to warm up to her.

Grace was like that. Charming and adventurous.

She might be nervous about heading off to Colorado with me, but she was doing it. I could see the light in her eyes. I could hope that I had contributed somewhat to that light, but I was fairly certain that she was excited about going to Whiskey Springs.

It was a lot more interesting than traveling to Tucson in a stagecoach.

Reaching her door, I knocked first. When there was no answer I called out her name.

Then knocked again.

I even leaned my ear against the door, but heard nothing.

To hell with it.

I turned the knob and opened the door.

The bedroom was empty.

Thirty-Three

GRACE

After lunch, I went back to my bedroom while Lucas went out to hook up the horses. It had taken us quite a while to load up the wagon. There were things we were missing, but Lucas assured me that we could get whatever else we needed in El Paso if not some other waystation along the way.

He also agreed that it was a good idea for us to travel with others. It was a long, lonely trail to west and then north to Colorado. It would be good to have others around if we needed help.

This was wild territory even for a seasoned soldier.

I thought about Flora as I went outside and used the privy and wondered if I would ever see her again.

It was rather doubtful, but who knows. If nothing else, I would remember her and smile.

Going back inside, I made my way back to my bedroom where I had left my reticule.

I stepped inside the bedroom and froze.

I'd left my reticule on the bed.

But it wasn't there.

A quick glance around told I was in the right room. As did the one lone adolescent pine tree right outside the window.

Maybe Mrs. Tidwell thought I had forgotten it and took it with her to find me.

Or maybe Lucas had come looking for me.

Ready to see him again, I turned around, my skirts swishing around me and my heart lodged in my throat.

It was him. It was Blakely. The outlaw from the stagecoach. But he wasn't wearing his boiler hat. He actually looked completely different, but I recognized him by his cold black eyes.

"Did you miss me?" he asked.

I tried to make sense of his words. I almost looked over my shoulder to see who he was talking to. I'm sure I shook my head.

"Did you really think I was going to let you go?" he asked.

A little trill of panic shot up my spine. He was standing between me and the door.

"Why are you here? I don't know you."

"We're going to enjoy getting to know each other."

I looked to my left. There was a window, but I couldn't get it open and get through it without the risk of him stopping me.

Since I didn't see a way to escape, I brought myself up to my full five feet two inches and faced him head on.

"I'm going to leave now," I said. "And you're going to forget that you ever met me."

"No need to get testy," he said with a calmness that was eerie in itself.

"Lucas will be looking for me."

"He's busy with that wagon. He'll be awhile."

"I'm leaving." I took a step forward.

He held up my reticule.

"Why do you have that?" I asked. "that's mine."

"You've collected quite a sum of money for yourself."

I kept my face blank, but my heart sank. I always kept my money in the little money pouch I wore around my waist. I had designed it myself.

I always kept my money on my person.

But not today.

Today I had put my money in my reticule when I had changed dresses.

I held out my hand. "Give me that. It's mine."

"I don't think so."

"Fine," I said. "If you're pathetic enough to steal from a woman, just take it."

I walked forward, determined to get around him, but he put a hand on my arm to stop me. His grasp was not gentle by a long shot. His fingernail dug through the thin cotton of my dress into my skin.

"Stop it," I said. "You're hurting me."

"You might as well get used to a little pain," he said.

Gasping, I jerked back and looked into his black eyes.

Then I fought him.

When that didn't work, I went to scream, but he clamped a hand over my mouth. But it wasn't just his hand. It was a sweet smelling cloth.

I tried to hold my breath as I continued to break free of his hold, but it wasn't working.

The sweet smell was seeping into my lungs.

Then I felt myself fading.

I was losing consciousness and losing it quickly. My strength was waning. I couldn't hold him at bay any longer.

"Lucas," I said, though it might not have been out loud.

Then everything went blank.

Thirty-Four

LUCAS

"Where is Grace?" I demanded of Mrs. Tidwell. She was in the kitchen rolling out some dough with a wooden rolling pin.

Mrs. Tidwell looked up at me, her expression much too calm for my taste.

"I thought she had gone with you."

"Well, she didn't."

"I haven't seen her," she said, going back to her kneading.

There was a bowl full of peeled and cut apples in a bowl on the table to her left.

It occurred to me that she was making an apple pie. Such an inconsequential thing, yet she saw it as being more important than locating Grace.

"She went to her room," I said. "Now she's gone."

Mrs. Tidwell shrugged. "Maybe she decided to leave on her own."

That comment brought me up short.

Even though I had no choice but to consider the possibility, I quickly dismissed it.

Grace wouldn't do that.

Not a chance.

"She's here. Somewhere," I said.

"If I see her, I'll let you know that you're looking for her," she said, sprinkling more flour over the clump of dough.

I shook my head. This would not do.

"I'll tear this house apart. This town apart. Until I find her."

Mrs. Tidwell stopped her kneading and looked at me as she wiped her hands on her apron. "Be my guest," she said.

So I did just that. I went through each and every room of her house. Even her private rooms. I went outside. I looked for her everywhere.

I even went back out to the wagon, tore back the canvas, and looked inside it. Nothing. I barged into the General Store. Made a sweep around the store, checking behind tables stacked with bolts of cloth and candles and bags of beans. Walked a path among barrels of flour and cracker boxes.

Going up to the storekeeper who reeked of peppermint he had snagged from the glass jar on the counter, I put my hands on the counter and leaned toward him.

"Have you seen Grace? The young lady who was with me all morning?"

"No, Sir," he said. "I haven't seen Miss Grace since she left here with you."

"God damn it," I said under my breath. Then to the storekeeper. "Are you certain?"

"I'm certain."

"Have you seen anyone else come into town? Anyone new?" I don't even know why I asked that. It was the Texas Ranger in me.

"No, Sir," he said. "You might check with the livery."

"The livery." Without another word, I turned around and strode purposely from the room.

Grace was nowhere to be found. With each place I came up empty-handed, the sick feeling in the pit of my stomach got heavier and heavier.

I wasn't leaving here until I found her.

It wasn't far to the livery, but it seemed to take forever to cross the street and cover the hundred yards or so to it. The wind, dry and gritty, stung my skin and got into my eyes.

The barn looked empty at first, then I saw a lad brushing a sturdy chestnut colored horse.

"Hey," I said. "Have you seen a young lady? Pretty. Wearing a light blue dress?"

"No Sir," he said, shoving his old brown derby hat back. "Not in here."

"Anywhere?" I asked.

"Out at the wagon. I think she was with you."

"But you haven't seen her since then?"

"No sir." He lifted one of the horse's hooves to examine it.

I turned around, facing the door again.

Someone had to have seen her. She hadn't just vanished. Hell, she didn't even have her own horse.

A couple of men, tired and dirty, rode past, looking like they'd been riding all day. They tied their horses to the hitching post at the General Store and, after dismounting, went inside.

Strangers. Something clicked in the back of my mind. Something that made me feel like I'd just been hit in the gut. I turned around again.

The lad had moved on to the next hoof.

"What about anyone else?" I asked. "A stranger?"

The lad straightened. "There was a man. About your size. He came and got his horse less than an hour ago. Seemed like he was in quite a hurry."

"Did he say what his name was?"

"Didn't say. And I didn't ask."

"Anything else you noticed about him? Anything unusual?"

The boy scratched his head. Lifted his hat and lowered it again. "There was one thing."

I waited, dreading his answer, though I couldn't imagine what it might be.

"He wore a pocket watch in the inside pocket of his jacket. It was a bright silver. Reflected the light like a mirror."

There was that feeling again. Helpless dread.

"Which way did he go?"

The boy shrugged and went to working on the horse's hoof. "Couldn't say. Like I said, he left like he was in a hurry."

Turning around , I stepped back outside.

I looked down the street in one direction, then looked in the other direction.

There was nothing unusual to see except for a tumbleweed rolling past by the dry wind.

He had been here.

Blakely had been here.

And I would bet my life that he had Grace.

The son-of-a-bitch was going to pay for this one.

If he hurt so much as a hair on Grace's head, it would be the last thing he did.

GRACE

I woke with the light of a lantern across my face and the scent of something vile cooking. The smell reminded me of a freshly skinned squirrel one of the Amirault brothers had brought to the kitchen.

I'd taken one whiff, ran outside, and gagged. It was the worst scent I had ever smelled and I had never forgotten it. Just thinking about it could make me queasy.

Maybe this was hell.

In all truthfulness, I had no idea where I was.

When I moved to turn over, everything hurt. Inside and out. My hair covered my face, but I didn't even have the wherewithal to move it aside.

So I just lay there, letting the seconds flow past as I searched my memories for some explanation. I had none.

When I tried to open my eyes, I decided it was good that my hair covered my face. Even my eyes hurt, especially with the light in them.

I managed to move a hand just enough to reach the edge of the mattress. Just a few more inches and I confirmed my suspicion. The thin mattress was on the floor or maybe it was the ground. I couldn't be sure.

A metal spoon struck against an iron pot making the vile scent even stronger. Someone was stirring something in a pot over a fire. I could hear the faint sound of the flames crackling as they devoured the wood.

I tried to remember how I got here, wherever this was.

I remembered helping Lucas pack the wagon. We were getting ready go west. Then north.

After that, I only saw flashes of memories. Lunch. Ham and bread. I'd gone to my room.

Why had I gone to my room? I couldn't remember.

"I know you're awake."

The voice chilled me to the bone.

It was Blakely.

Then I remembered. Blakely had been in my room.

All I remembered was seeing him standing there. Holding my reticule.

And somehow I was with him now.

I used all my strength, pushing past the pain, and forced myself to sit up.

We were in the woods. Nothing but darkness all around us.

We sat in a circle of light created by the fire and the lantern that was in my eyes.

I'd been right. He had a pot hanging over the open fire.

"You're a lucky lady," he said. "I don't cook for just anybody."

He might call that cooking, but I wanted nothing to do with it. I wasn't about to eat anything he gave me no matter how much my stomach grumbled. And I certainly wasn't going to eat something that smelled like a freshly skinned squirrel.

He picked up a flask and tossed it so that it landed beside me.

"Where are we?" I asked, but my throat was dry and it was hard to talk.

I picked up the flask and drank. I might not eat his food, but I had no choice but to drink his water.

"Somewhere no one will find us," he said, answering my first question.

"Why?" I asked, securing the lid back on the flask.

"I'm taking you with me," he said.

"Taking me where?"

"On a need to know basis."

"Why?" I asked again.

"Because the Texas Ranger likes you. He'll come after you. And when he does, we'll be ready for him."

"Who is we?" I asked.

"You'll find out soon enough," he said, dipping a spoon into the pot and filling a bowl.

He slid it over next to me.

It looked as vile as it smelled.

I turned away, covering my nose with my sleeve, trying not to gag.

"You can be uppity if you want to, but this is what you're getting to eat."

"What is it?" I asked, not really wanting to know.

"Squirrel liver," he said.

Turning away, I nearly gagged. Would have gagged, but I wasn't going to let him see my weakness.

I looked into his coal black eyes. That certainly explained the smell.

There was no way I was going to put any of that in my mouth. I'd starve to death first.

What I needed to know was how long I'd been out here.

Did Lucas know I was missing yet?

If he did, he would come looking for me. He would find me.

This Blakely fellow must have brought me out here on a horse. That explained why everything hurt.

We couldn't have gotten very far. Not riding with me unconscious.

"Where are you taking me?" I asked.

He didn't answer, of course.

I needed to know where we were. If I knew where we were, maybe I could escape and I would know which direction to go.

"I need to use the privy," I said.

"Of course you do."

But he got up and held out a hand to help me up.

I looked down my nose at his hand and stood up by myself.

I didn't want his food or his help. As far as I was concerned he was nothing.

As I walked away from the fire, I decided that escaping in the middle of the night would be downright foolhardy. There were wolves and all sorts of other wild animals that would love to eat me for dinner.

"That's far enough," Blakely called.

As much as I hated to agree with him on anything, I had to admit that he was right about that.

I would wait. I would bide my time.

But I would escape this man.

In the meantime, Lucas would be looking for me.

Blakely would not win whatever game it was that he was playing.

Thirty-Six

LUCAS

I saddled Sparky and led him out of the barn.

It was going to be dark soon. And with darkness I had a much lower chance of finding them.

Blakely had Grace. There was no other explanation.

Why? I couldn't say.

I had two choices. East or west.

I'd asked around. I must have asked every person who lived in Miller's Creek. Finally I got lucky.

A farmer on the edge of town, on the west side, had seen a man riding past a couple of hours ago. He couldn't say for sure, but he thought it odd that the man carried a lady wearing a light blue dress in front of him.

She'd looked to be asleep or unconscious. Whatever it was, it didn't look natural. But the farmer hadn't felt it his place to interfere. Not when it could be something simple like a man carrying his young daughter. All he could really see for sure was the light blue dress.

At least I knew I was heading in the right direction. I rode slowly, looking for any signs whatsoever that they had left the road.

I'd never claimed to be a good tracker. We had soldiers who could do that, some better than others.

Even so, I could hold my own. That was especially true with Grace's life on the line.

The man had just boldly come to the inn and swiped her right from under my nose.

He was bold, I'd say that for him.

As I rode, watching the sun getting ready to drop, I tried to make sense of it all.

I just couldn't understand why Blakely would take Grace.

What good could she possible be to him?

He was planning on violating her, he might as well get ready to have his insides ripped out. I'd learned a thing or two from the Indians that I had never expected would come in handy.

Might just rip his fingernails out, too, just for good measure.

Any man who hurt a woman didn't deserve to live.

And right now I had no empathy for the man. He wasn't going to pull something like this and live to stand before a judge.

What I didn't understand was why. Why would he take Grace?

All I knew was a general direction. After that all bets were off.

A man could hide behind one of the knolls around here. One of those dips that no one could see until they right up on it. They could do whatever they wanted to do. No one would ever know.

It was possible that I would go to my grave without finding her.

Nonetheless, I was prepared to do just that. I needed to enlist some help from the Texas Rangers. And I would, but I didn't have time to wait for them to get the message and to get here.

No matter what, I would never stop looking for her.

No matter how long it took, I would never stop searching for her.

I couldn't. Grace was going to be my wife.

She might not know it just yet, but she'd get on board soon enough.

This more than proved my point. A woman out here needed protection.

I tried not to think about how the man had stolen her right out from beneath my nose.

GRACE

About an hour, by my best guess, Blakely stretched out on his bedroll, closed his eyes, and promptly started snoring.

I wasn't bound. Nor was I drugged.

He obviously wasn't worried about me getting away. No person in their right mind would leave the safety of the fire. Not when they had no idea where they were other than out here in the middle of nowhere.

As I lay there contemplating my predicament, I listened to a pack of wolves howling.

It hadn't taken long to figure out that we were outside. I'd known that the minute I'd gone just outside the circle of light created by the fire.

The wind was gritty and warm, even in the darkness. A precursor to the heat of summer on its way.

I could still smell the squirrel liver soup Blakely had tried to feed me. He'd poured it back in the pot after it became clear that I wasn't going to eat it.

I wasn't good at telling time by the moon. I had never slept outside before and did not plan on making it a habit.

With daybreak, I would get my bearings. I would be able to tell by the sun which direction we were traveling.

Lucas may not be able to find me, but I would escape Blakely. I would find my way back to Lucas.

He was the man I was going to marry. It had taken me my whole adult life to find him and I was not going to let him go easily.

He hadn't asked me to marry him, but he would come around. He'd promised to take care of me.

My eyes watered as I remembered the fierceness in his eyes when he'd made that declaration.

It occurred to me then, starting as a tiny spark of a thought, that Lucas might think I had run away from him. He might think I had changed my mind and decided to run away from him.

That was the last thing I wanted to do, but he wouldn't know that.

I had not told him how I felt.

I'd been waiting to see how he felt about me.

But I knew that. He'd told me.

I was the one who hadn't said anything.

If he thought I had run away from him, then he wouldn't look for me.

The thought had me sick to my stomach.

It wasn't that I was afraid for myself. I could get away from Blakely.

It made me sick that he could think that I had left because I didn't want to go west with him. That I didn't want to be with him.

It made me sick because that was the farthest thing from my mind.

I was very much looking forward to going to Colorado with him.

My only concern was that I didn't think it wise that we travel alone, just in case something happened. If he got sick or hurt, then I would left to tend to the horses, to make sure the wagon was in good order or even to fix it if something went wrong.

I was a lady's maid. I knew fashion and etiquette. I could speak French fluently and even some Latin.

This was not my world. I could make it my world, but not alone. Not in the desert.

When the wolves stopped howling, I shivered. When they were howling, I at least knew where they were.

Blakely continued to snore.

I wondered where his gun was. If I could get my hands on his gun...

No. I dismissed the thought. It was my job to stay alive.

That was it. Just stay alive.

But I would not eat squirrel liver to do it.

Thirty-Eight

LUCAS

I stopped when darkness fell. Not because I wanted to and not because I was giving up, but because traveling in the darkness, I risked missing any signs of their trail.

I tethered my horse and made a small fire. I had biscuits in my haversack, but I needed the fire to ward off the wolves.

Stretching out on my bed roll, I rested my head on my arms behind my head.

Wolves howled in the distance. This was wild untamed country, not to be taken lightly.

Not sleepy, I stared at the moon.

Stared at the moon and thought about Grace.

I refused to consider what I would do if I couldn't find her.

Not finding her was not an option.

I would find her.

Once I found her, we would continue our way forward to Colorado.

We would make a home there. I'd build her a house and we would fill it with children.

Most Texas Rangers gave up any semblance of a normal life.

Once we reached our destination, I'd send a letter letting my commanding officer know that I left Texas.

The one thing we wouldn't have to worry about would be money.

Everything was arranged for me to stop in Denver, take care of my business, then we were free to do as we pleased.

I still didn't know about her or her past, but those things didn't matter to me. She didn't know the things I had done in my past and I didn't plan on telling her.

Some things were left in the past.

The wolves quieted.

After listening to the silence for a few minutes, I pulled my pistol out of my holster and held it on my chest.

I moved my attention to listening to sounds that might indicate the wolves were near. I watched for their shining eyes in the darkness.

I most preferred the wolves when they howled.

When they were quiet, they could be dangerous.

If I couldn't keep myself alive, I was of no use to Grace.

The thought of Blakely putting a single hand on her made my blood boil.

And yet I already knew that he had ridden away with her.

I hadn't heard where his gang was. For some reason he was separated from them.

That was troubling.

Blakely separated from his gang was akin to the wolves going quiet.

Both were equally troubling.

I should have sent for help before setting off after them. I had been blinded by thoughts of rescuing Grace. That had been my objective.

But if I ran into Blakely's gang, there could be trouble.

I wasn't concerned for myself so much.

I was concerned for Grace. Everything could so easily go sideways with me trying to fight a gang of outlaws while keeping her safe.

Didn't matter.

I would do whatever it took.

A Texas Ranger did not hesitate to protect those he loved.

Thirty-Nine

GRACE

"Wake up."

I had finally dozed, my body forcing me to sleep.

I jerked awake at the sound of Blakely's voice.

He kicked at the fire, not caring that he sent ashes my way, staining my dress.

He cared about nothing other than himself.

I sat up and rubbed my eyes.

It was still dark. Just light enough that I could see my hands in front of my face without the fire or the lantern, both of which Blakely had put out.

The sun would be up shortly.

"Where are we going?" I asked, persisting, hoping he would slip and tell me something.

"Not your concern."

I bit my tongue. It was every bit my concern. Wherever he was taking me, it was against my will.

Still. I had to bide my time.

I had to choose the right time to bolt.

"Go on," he said. "Take your privacy. Don't even think about running. There's nowhere for you to go. You'll die out here by yourself.

I rolled my eyes in answer to him, but he didn't even notice. He was busy saddling his horse. I was inconsequential to him. A means to an end.

"Get on the horse," he said ten minutes later.

"I'll walk," I said.

"No," he said. "You won't."

He stood a good head taller than me and I had to look up to see into his eyes. His cold black eyes.

I saw apathy in them. Maybe even evil.

Whatever it was, it chilled me and reminded me to bide my time.

Stay alive.

Either I would escape or Lucas would find me. Either way, all I had to do was to survive.

I held on tightly to the saddle horn as he nudged the horse into a walk.

West, I decided. We were headed west.

We were riding into the darkness and the sun was coming up behind us.

He was right. We were in the middle of nowhere.

As the sun continued to rise, I saw nothing but rolling hills and cacti.

The main road could be to our south or our north.

That part I couldn't tell.

Eventually we would reach wherever it was he was taking me. In the meantime I would wait. He'd said it himself. He needed me.

My stomach grumbled with hunger.

It didn't matter where he was taking me. It was going to be a long ride.

But I was strong. I could withstand.

I focused my thoughts instead on Lucas. Let myself picture him coming after me. Following our trail.

He needed a way to follow. Perhaps he would find the fire and that would lead him closer toward us.

If I had something I could leave as a trail, I would do so, but I had nothing.

All I had was my faith.

My faith in Lucas and my faith in myself.

Forty

LUCAS

I knelt next to what had been a fire. Someone had covered it with dirt, but it had clearly been a fire and still had some warmth to it.

They had also cooked something that smelled especially vile. I just hoped that whatever it was Grace hadn't been expected to eat it.

She was a lady and a lady couldn't possibly be expected to eat what smelled like rat guts.

The trail I'd followed wasn't far off the road. It, in fact, ran parallel to the main road.

Blakely would be trying to stay out of sight, but he wasn't getting far from the main road. He might present with bravado, but in the end, he took few risks.

I wasn't far behind them. They had probably, like me, left at the first light of day.

My best guess was that I was about two hours behind them.

I only saw one set of horse tracks. No footprints. Blakely had her on the horse with him.

As I nudged my horse into a gallop, I imagined all the things I could do to torture him.

There were so many possibilities.

Mostly I just wanted to kick his ass.

I would do that in addition to pulling out his fingernails and ripping his insides out.

But only after I found Grace and she was safe.

That was my first priority.

Once the sun started coming up, it took no time for the sky to brighten.

I squinted to see ahead, but, of course, I couldn't see Blakely or Grace.

There were too many dips and knolls in a land that a man couldn't even see until he was upon them.

It was a strange land. One I knew far too well.

I wouldn't miss it, though. I wouldn't miss the blistering heat and the miles and miles and miles of nothing.

I wouldn't miss the rattlesnakes or the wolves or any of the other hazards, so many a man couldn't even begin to prepare for all of them.

After about ten minutes of riding, I lost their trail.

I pushed forward anyway. They couldn't be far away.

Then I saw a little shack up ahead. It looked like someone had thrown some boards up, slapped a roof on it, then left it to weather to a worn gray.

I saw its roof first, then the rest of it came into sight. A few minutes later, I saw the horse.

Slowing Sparky, I went on alert.

There was, of course, no way to slip up on the shack without being seen. No trees. Nothing to hide behind.

I pulled my rifle out of the sleeve and laid it across my lap. Then I pulled my pistol out of the holster and gripped it in my hand.

There was no good way to do this.

Sparky neighed and I patted him on the neck.

There had to be a better way.

I slid off the horse and tied his reins to what passed for a hitching post.

With a rifle in one hand and my pistol in the other, I crept up to the shack.

Leaning against the old worn wood, I stood very quietly. Waiting. Waiting and listening.

I heard no sounds coming from inside.

I slowly began to relax.

When the first crack of wood slammed me over the head, I tried to turn around. To see my attacker. But then the second one hit and it knocked me down.

Everything went black.

Forty-One

I must have done something to alert Blakely that my primary thought at the moment was escaping.

Everything was good until we reached what he called Prickly Pear Point. Prickly Pear Point was nothing more than a shack. A shack made from old wood weathered to a fine gray. It was impossible to say if the shack had been built from old wood, then weathered or if had already been weathered before it was thrown up in some semblance of what looked more like a chicken coop than what Blakely called a cabin.

Once we were inside the shack, he decided to tie my hands behind my back with a frayed piece of hemp rope. I sat on the dirt floor with my hands tied behind my back.

The shack had one chair and Blakely sat in it.

We had no more than gotten situated into what looked like was going to be a long day, when I heard a horse and rider approaching. I blamed myself for what happened next.

I don't think Blakely heard the horse, but I looked toward the direction of the welcomed sound, alerting him.

He went to peer through a slit in the wall. He grinned slowly.

"What is it?" I asked.

"Shut the hell up," he growled.

I wasn't surprised when he clamped a cloth around my mouth and tied it behind my head.

It had to be Lucas. If it was Blakely's men, he wouldn't be concerned about keeping me quiet.

I watched in horror as he moved stealthily across the room and slid out the door.

I heard the crack of wood over the man's head.

I stood up and tried to walk toward the door. To warn Lucas. It wasn't easy standing up from the floor with my hands tied behind my back, especially with my long skirts hindering my progress. But I would do it for Lucas.

When I heard the second crack of wood, I knew that was it.

The man crumpled to the ground.

I made it to the wall and looked out through a crack—they were everywhere—in between the planks.

Lucas lay on the ground, unconscious. I spit out the cloth Blakely had hastily and carelessly tied around my mouth.

"Lucas!"

I ran toward the door and that was when I realized that Blakely had tied my ankle to a post. I tugged on it. It wouldn't take much to pull the post down, probably bringing down the whole shack.

But before I could do that, Blakely reached the door, dragging Lucas behind him.

Blakely wore a smug expression. "I told you he'd come for you."

He deposited Lucas on the dirt floor. I didn't even bother

responding to Blakely. Instead I went right to Lucas, kneeling next to him.

Blakely didn't try to stop me. He went back to his chair and pulled out a cigar.

I couldn't help Lucas with my hands tied behind me.

"Untie me," I said, looking over my shoulder.

"Not happening," he said.

Since I couldn't help him, I laid down beside him, my head on his chest and let the tears fall unchecked.

Lucas had come for me.

He had come, but Blakely had knocked him out.

Lucas was still breathing though. As long as I could feel his chest moving beneath my cheek, I had hope.

LUCAS

I woke with a splitting headache. A headache and a pressure on my chest.

I immediately knew where I was. I was in the shack with Blakely.

It took me a little longer to figure out that the pressure on my chest was Grace, lying on top of me.

Without moving anything other than my eyes, I took in the situation.

Blakely sat in a chair, smoking a cigar, staring out the open door. He looked like he was waiting for something. Someone.

Grace lay with her head on my chest and it didn't take long to figure out that she was asleep. My shirt was damp with her tears, but she was sleeping peacefully now.

I didn't see any of Blakely's gang. It was just him. Probably who he waited for.

"Grace," I whispered.

When she didn't answer, I put a hand on the back of her head.

With a sharp intake of breath, she opened her eyes and lifted her head.

"Shh," I said, keeping one eye on Blakely. He seemed completely unconcerned with us as he blew a smoke ring into the air.

She lowered her head and whispered in my ear. "Are you okay?"

"No," I whispered back. "But I'm alive."

"My hands are tied," she said.

I stretched my own hands. I wasn't tied. And since I wasn't tied, I had every reason to believe that we were going to get out of this.

"Wait," I said, the one word full of caution.

She laid her head back on my chest and the seconds turned into minutes.

Blakely, finally, got up to go outside.

"We have to get out of here," I whispered unnecessarily.

"How?"

"Roll off me. Onto your stomach."

She did as I asked.

I reached into my pocket and, pulling out my knife, sliced through the rope holding her hands tied.

She rubbed her wrists. The sight of her bruised skin had my blood boiling.

But I had to keep a level head.

What had Blakely done with my guns?

"Grace," I said. "You have to get out of here."

"I'm not leaving you."

"You have to. You have to go for help."

She was shaking her head.

"Yes. Sparky is tied outside. Get on him and ride south. You'll come to the main road. Follow it down the trail to Castle Rock."

"I'm not leaving you here," she said again.

"I'll be alright. If I know you're safe, I can take care of myself."

"You can ride," she said.

"He'll never let us both go.

"How do I get away?"

"Remember Flora?"

"Of course."

"Take a page from her book and tell him you need some privacy. Then go."

She was shaking her head again.

"It's the only way."

I looped the rope back around her bleeding wrists, but lightly enough that she could easily slip from the knots.

Forty-Three

GRACE

I had somehow fallen asleep with my head on Lucas's chest, but I woke with a start when I heard him calling my name.

Relief flooded through me that he was conscious again.

I had feared for his life.

The house was in shadows.

"You have to get out of here," he said. "You have to go for help."

"I won't leave you here."

"It's me he wants. Not you," he said. "He won't go after you."

"He'll kill you."

"Not a chance." The expression on his face was so severe, I was inclined to believe him. "Did he hurt you?"

"He drugged me and tied my wrists, but not other than that. He has my money."

"Alright," he said. "I needed to know that."

"Why?"

"You don't want to know."

"Let's just say depending on how much he hurt you, I have slow and painful torture planned for him."

"He's coming back," she said, dropping her head back on my chest.

"Tell him you need to go outside before it gets dark."

Blakely came back inside and sat back down in his chair.

It made sense. It was the least I could do for him, even if I did not want to leave him behind. Now that Blakely had Lucas, he had no more use for me.

I could do this.

I had no choice.

Lifting my head, I sat up.

"I have to use the privy," I said.

"There is no privy," Blakely said flatly.

"I can't help it." I got to my feet. "I have to have some privacy."

"Go on," he said, motioning with his cigar.

I darted for the door and took a minute to get my bearings.

The sun was headed down in the west.

East. Lucas wanted me to go east. To get to Castle Rock. Get help. There would be men there. Soldiers.

I reached Sparky.

Looking up, I wondered just how I was supposed to get up there.

Sparky was a big horse.

I ran my damp palms over my dress. Lucas had forgotten that I didn't even know how to ride a horse on my own. Lucas obviously had forgotten about that.

Unlooping the reins from the hitching post, I led Sparky away. We walked thus until we were out of sight of the shack. My heart was pounding in my chest.

If Blakely saw us...

A few steps more. It was so quiet out here. Thinking about how alone I was, in itself, was rather alarming.

It didn't make any sense for me to walk all the way to Castle Rock. I would take

entirely too long.

With one last glance over my shoulder, I put a foot in the stirrup and hoisted myself onto Sparky's back with an oomph.

I sat for a minute, getting my bearing from being on the back of the horse. I gripped the saddle horn like a lifeline.

Alone.

Talk about being forced whether to sink or swim.

I was in the deep end now.

I adjusted my skirts.

East. He wanted me to ride east.

The road was supposed to be nearby.

I just had to find it.

I had to get to Cactus Rock before darkfall.

It wasn't too much to ask.

Holding the reins tightly in one hand, keeping the other on the saddle horn I leaned low over Sparky's neck. "Help me out, boy," I said. "I don't know what to do."

Sparky took the initiative and began a slow, easy trot south.

Minutes later we reached the road just as Lucas had said we would.

I did as he instructed and turned right.

Cactus Rock.

Get to Cactus Rock. Get help. Get back to Lucas.

My memory flashed back to that morning so long ago when I had been out riding with my father.

But this wasn't morning. I wasn't six-years-old and Lucas needed me.

His life depended on my riding this horse to Cactus Rock and getting help.

I could do it.

I would do it.

"Let's go, Sparky," I said.

And off we went, like the wind.

Forty-Four

LUCAS

"Where is she?" Blakely asked.

"How should I know?"

Blakely paced around the small perimeter of the shack like a caged animal. He stopped after a bit and peered out through the cracks.

It was dark and there was no moon.

This was good that Blakely couldn't see, but bad for Grace.

Had she had time to get to Cactus Rock before the sun set?

"I don't see your horse," he said.

"It's dark."

Blakely turned and faced me accusingly.

"Her hands were tied."

"I wouldn't know." My head was seriously pounding. It felt like it was going to split in two.

Blakely went back to his chair.

I needed to distract Blakely away from Grace.

"Are you meeting your men here?"

"Not your business."

I shrugged, though he couldn't see me.

Blakely stood up and faced me in the darkness. Then he struck a match and lit a candle.

Bent down and held it close to my face.

"You know something," he said.

If he hadn't hit me over the head, I would have easily taken advantage of this situation.

But he was just out of my reach and I had no weapon.

Besides, I was just now realizing that he somehow pulled my right shoulder out of joint and it hurt like hell. I wasn't even sure I could use my right arm.

I was at a decided disadvantage.

It would be foolhardy to risk it and I was not a foolhardy man. I had sent Grace for help. I had to give her a chance. Otherwise it would be all for naught.

"What could I possibly know, Blakely?" I asked.

"I don't know yet." Blakely straightened and went back to his chair.

Wind whistled around the shack, the only thing in its path for miles, and wolves howled in the distance. This was a desolate place.

A place Blakely could hide out and no one would ever find him.

I only hoped Matthew had the wherewithal to find it.

I needed to come up with a backup plan just in case.

"Someone's coming," Blakely announced, dousing the candle.

Things were about to get interesting.

Either Blakey's men were showing up or my soldiers had found us.

If it was Blakely's men, I didn't stand a chance.

Not unless I did something.

Clamping my teeth together in an effort to distract myself from the searing pain in my shoulder, I stood up and stealthily made my way to the other side of the cabin.

Feeling my way, I wrapped my fingers around a rifle.

The sound of the horse's hooves was getting closer and closer.

Using all the strength I could muster, I lifted the rifle and stood behind Blakely.

I waited. As the horses got closer, the clouds shifted just enough that I could see Blakely's outline in the darkness.

I rammed the butt of the rifle into the back of his head. Once, then as he fell, I hit him again.

He fell loudly to the floor.

"Bastard." I muttered as I kicked him in the ribs.

The horses, whether friend or foe, I didn't know, were right outside. Crouching down, I inched over to the door and waited.

I listened closely for any sounds, voices, that might tell me who was out there in the darkness.

Had Grace made it in time?

Or was it Blakely's men?

Forty-Five

GRACE

The next day

The owner of the inn in Castle rock had insisted I take a bath and she had given me a dress to wear. It was a plain, serviceable dress, much like I had worn as Daphne's lady's maid.

It fit well enough and even more importantly, it was clean.

The inn was a two-story house, like most of the other inns along the Butterfield Stage Route. This one was bigger though, with a piano in the main dining room.

The owner of the inn, a young lady not much older than me, sat playing a lively tune. Her name was Claire and she ran this place by herself or so she told me.

Four men sat at a table playing cards.

The rest of the men, including the soldiers, had set off after I had arrived.

Matthew remembered me and he knew of Prickly Pear Point.

"Lucas is there," I told him. "he's injured."

The men had rallied and within fifteen minutes, very impressive in itself, had taken off in the direction I had come.

I soon learned from Claire that Blakely's men had been arrested and were behind bars across the street in the jail.

From her account, it wasn't much of a jail and the townspeople were anxiously awaiting tomorrow when a group of soldiers would be escorting them to El Paso, far away from their little community.

The lively music seemed to mock my anxious mood.

I had left Lucas alone with Blakely, not that I could have done anything to help him, and I had actually made it here on horseback to get help for him.

I was rather pleased with myself for riding this way on horseback. By myself.

Sparkly hadn't seemed to need me to do much at all. It was almost like he understood what I was doing.

I might not become an avid rider anytime in my future, but I wouldn't have the same fear of riding that I'd had most of my life.

I paced the room from one end to the other.

The music stopped and Claire came up to me.

"Grace," she said. "Can I ask a favor of you?"

"Of course," I said. I was beholden to Claire for helping me. Giving me clean clothes and a safe place to stay.

"I have to take care of some things. Would you play the piano until I get back?"

"Oh." A shot of nerves shot through me. "It's been so long since I touched a piano."

It had in fact been since I was fifteen when my mother had been forced to sell our piano.

"Please," she said. "I don't want to leave the men with silence."

"Okay," I said. "But no promises that I'll be any good."

As I walked to the piano, it occurred to me to wonder how she had known I even knew how to play. Perhaps it had simply been an assumption.

I sat at the piano and lightly rested my fingers on the keys. I had been well-practiced in piano. It was one of the many things I had been taught as a child and teenager.

I had never dared play around Daphne. Daphne played as did her sisters, but no one had ever seemed to give a thought that I might know how and truly, why would they?

I was a lady's maid, after all, and no one expected me to have been taught the things that a lady had.

There were only four men here to hear me. They were focused on their card game and I doubted they would even notice anything I might play.

Taking a deep breath, I closed my eyes and let my fingers go.

I played. I started with a simple song, warming up my fingers. Then they seemed to move of their own accord, everything I had learned rushing back to me.

It was a reminder that at my core, I was a lady, cultured and refined.

It had merely been suppressed for a few years.

I lost myself in the music, playing my heart out.

I don't even know how long I played.

When I opened my eyes, the four men who had been playing cards were standing a few feet away from me, listening. They looked pleased and not a little pleasantly surprised. Claire was there, too, a rather smug expression on her face.

I smiled, but I kept playing, my eyes half closed, moving into a sadder, more romantic song that matched my mood.

As I played, someone came up behind the men and they shifted to let him through.

My heart rate increased, sensing something my conscious mind didn't.

My hands were still flying over the keys, but my gaze shifted to the man who had just arrived.

I gasped and my fingers slowed, then stopped abruptly, leaving discordant notes hanging in the air.

Lucas stood there. He looked so handsome. He had a white sling across his shoulder, but he was wearing clean clothes and he had shaved.

He smiled at me and started toward me.

Without even thinking, I stood up and walked toward him as well.

Seconds later I was in his arms.

"You're okay," I said, pulling back to look into his eyes.

"I'm more than okay," he said.

Then he kissed me.

Epilogue

Grace

The next month

I sat next to Lucas on the buckboard of our Conestoga wagon.

He had the reins.

If I'd thought the stagecoach was bumpy, I'd had no idea what bumpy was until I rode across the desert in a wagon. I held onto the sides of the wooden seat as we hit another hole in the path that served as a road.

We were fifth in line in the wagon train.

Behind us, it stretched as far as the eye could see like a wavy line of white.

In front of us stood the mountains.

We'd been moving slowly toward them, ever so slowly, closer and closer, over the past two days.

I'd begun to think that we would never reach them.

I told Lucas.

"We'll be there before you know it."

"How do you know that?" I asked, narrowing my eyes at him. "You've never been here."

"Because I'm a very wise man."

I smiled and gazed over at him.

He was a wise man. A good man.

"Tell me again where we're going," I said. I knew, of course, but I liked to hear him tell me about it. I think he knew it.

"Whiskey Springs," he said, never tiring of telling me. "Deep in the heart of the Rocky Mountains." He looked over at me.

I smiled.

"You know," he said. "They say there's a magic in Whiskey Springs. That it brings people together. Soul mates."

"Is that so?" I asked.

"It's what they say."

"Then I suppose you should be careful, lest someone think he's my soul mate once we get there."

He took my hand and kissed the back of my fingers.

"I don't think you have to worry about that," he said. "You've already met your soul mate."

"Is that so?" I asked, looking at him from beneath my lashes.

"That is so," he said.

"How will I know him?"

"He'll be the one at your side, day and night."

"I have you for that, Lucas," I said, smiling over at him and adjusting my skirts.

"That is absolutely true."

I looked at the little gold band on my left ring finger.

"It wouldn't matter anyway," I said. "I am a married woman, after all."

"Yes. And I know for a certainty that your husband is the luckiest man alive. Lucky and wise. He wouldn't do anything to risk losing you."

"Nor I you," I said.

The sunset would soon be washing the sky in a blur of reds and oranges.

We would be stopping soon. Circling our wagons.

Then when darkness came and quiet settled over the wagons, I would be tucked safely in the arms of the one man I loved above all others.

My very own Texas Ranger, Captain Lucas Roberts.

It mattered not to me where we went as long as we were together.

Keep Reading for a Preview of Finding Natalie...

KATHRYN KALEIGH

Finding Natalie

WHISKEY SPRINGS SERIES

Finding Natalie

PREVIEW

CHAPTER 1

1864

There was something magical about a snowy morning.

The world was quiet and peaceful.

Absolutely no sounds whatsoever. Like a soft blanket insulating the earth.

Quiet except for Biscuit's soft snoring. The dog was curled up on the foot of her bed, keeping her feet warm.

Biscuit was a big gangly black dog. He'd shown up on their doorstep about a year ago, just a puppy then. He still acted like a puppy, but was in a grown dog's body.

Natalie Worthington rolled over and looked out the window. The snow was still coming down like heavy rain.

Pulling the blankets up beneath her chin, she considered the possibility of staying in bed all day.

Less than four long years ago, she could have done it. That was before her father had left for the war and her mother was still alive.

But now her nine-year-old brother, Declan, was asleep down the hall and it was her responsibility to make sure he was fed and did his chores.

Finding enough food for him to eat was a full-time job.

The two of them worked from sunup to sundown just trying to survive.

Declan had gotten good at chopping firewood and liked to be outside.

Even today with the snow coming down, he'd see going outside to gather firewood as a grand adventure.

Unfortunately, that left Natalie with a world of other things to do. Like making sure Declan had dry clothes.

And lots of food to eat.

The Yankees had been through here about six months ago.

No matter what Doc said, Natalie believed that having the Yankees sitting on her settee was what sent her mother to her grave.

The Yankees had been cordial enough and had been respectful enough — contrary to the stories she'd heard about the havoc the enemy sometimes wreaked. Unfortunately, war was still war.

But without the war and their dreaded blue uniforms, the captain and his men would have been welcome guests in their home.

They had taken over the downstairs part of the house, leaving Natalie, her brother, and her mother privacy in the upstairs part.

It hadn't done them much good though. The kitchen was a separate building from the house. A feature common to all southern houses of any size.

So Natalie and her little family had to go downstairs and out the back door to get to the kitchen. That meant that every time her mother walked past the parlor, she saw the enemy lounging on her good furniture.

After the first day of making the trip to the kitchen outside, they'd started hoarding food upstairs to avoid walking past the soldiers three times a day.

The Yankees had been in the house for four days.

Mother had taken sick the same day the Yankees had marched away.

Natalie would have gone into town for the doctor, but the soldiers took the one horse they had left.

War was war.

So she'd sent Declan to the neighbor's house and asked them to send for the doctor.

When the doctor got there two days later, it was too late.

The doctor said it was her heart.

That it wasn't something sudden.

It didn't matter what the doc said, Natalie would go to her own grave knowing it was having Yankees in the house that had killed her. Her mother hadn't been able to see past the blue uniform.

And the knowledge that her husband was out there somewhere, most likely fighting against men wearing the same color uniform.

Natalie tossed the blankets aside and put her feet on the cold floor.

Shivering, she found her slippers, slipped them on, and wrapped her heavy cloak around her.

She needed to go out to the kitchen and get the fire going for breakfast.

Most days she went by herself out to the kitchen and made breakfast.

But today, she was reluctant to leave without Declan.

She tiptoed down the wide hallway and peeked into her brother's room.

"Declan?"

One thing she'd learned. Nine-year-old boys could sleep like the dead.

She went over and shook her brother.

He sat up, his eyes wide. "What's wrong?"

"Nothing," she said quickly. "It's snowing. We need to get to the kitchen before we get snowed in here."

He wiped at his eyes and nodded.

Natalie went back to her own room to get dressed.

She splashed cold water on her face and immediately regretted it as she shivered from the cold water.

She put on her warmest wool dress, thick socks, and her boots. Then put her cloak back on.

She ran a brush through her hair and was ready for the day. Or at least as ready as she was going to be.

She met her brother in the hall. He, too, was wearing warm clothes and a cloak.

"We'll come back later today and get all our blankets," she said. "We need to start sleeping in the kitchen. It'll be easier to keep warm."

"All right," Declan said.

She knew Declan didn't care one way or the other.

As long as he had plenty to eat and a warm place to sleep at night, not much else mattered.

He had a sadness about him now that was unnatural on a nine-year-old boy.

But it couldn't be helped.

It was the world they lived in.

Natalie focused on just surviving.

They'd survived a Yankee invasion and the loss of their parents. Now they needed to survive the first winter on their own.

They could do it.

Natalie just had to remember everything their parents had done and everything they'd been taught.

Natalie and Declan had done some fast growing up in these four years since the war started and even more since losing their mother.

But she was determined to keep the two of them alive.

Whatever it took.

And today it took moving them out of the big house into the kitchen. Fortunately, the kitchen was as big as many people's cabins, so it would be so much easier to stay warm in there.

The kitchen had actually become an integral part of their lives. A big stone fireplace for cooking and heating water. They even kept the cast iron bathtub in there so they didn't have to haul hot water to the house.

Walking together, Biscuit following along at their heels, they made their way down the hallway, down the stairs, and looked at each other before going outside.

"Ready?" she asked.

"No," Declan said.

But he opened the door anyway.

And they stepped outside into the snowstorm.

It was times like this that Natalie wished her grandfather had built a small cabin for them to live in instead of a grand manor house.

In a cabin, the kitchen would have been inside the house. A much simpler life than tramping through a snow storm... or a rain storm just to get something to eat.

Natalie put her head down as they walked the hundred yards or so to the kitchen.

Biscuit darted around them in his gangly way, stirring up even more clouds of snow.

About halfway to the kitchen, Natalie stopped and, shading her eyes, peered through the snow.

She smelled wood smoke.

There was already smoke coming from the kitchen's chimney.

She thought back to last night. Had they accidentally left enough wood in the fireplace that had kept burning all night?

No. Not possible. She was very careful about extinguishing the fire before they left the kitchen at night. They couldn't afford to have the kitchen burn down.

"There's somebody in the kitchen," Declan said.

"Wait." Natalie put a hand on his shoulder to hold him back.

It could be Yankees. Or worse. It could be southern renegades.

It would be just the worst luck to survive a Yankee invasion only for them to be taken down by renegades.

Renegades were far more dangerous than soldiers. Soldiers had a code.

Renegades had no code. No honor.

Biscuit took off, running toward the kitchen door. Natalie had to hold Declan back with both hands to keep him from going after the dog.

Even though Biscuit sometimes slept on her bed, Biscuit followed Declan around all day. As far as either of them were concerned, Biscuit was Declan's dog.

"We'll look in the window," she said.

They made their way through the falling snow to the window on this side of the kitchen.

Natalie held a finger up to her lips as they reached the window.

They peered in through the window, but the glass was fogged over.

All Natalie could see was a blazing fire in the fireplace.

She blinked away the snowflakes on her eyelashes and squinted to look closer.

There was a man sitting in front of the fireplace, just off to one side.

He was a Confederate soldier. Natalie could tell immediately by how tattered he looked.

It wasn't just his tattered uniform that she recognized. She recognized the hunched shoulders and defeated stance even from here.

But he wasn't close enough for her to recognize his features.

"We have to go back to the house," she said.

Declan nodded. "Are we gonna shoot him?"

"Are we gonna…" She started to tell him to watch his mouth. Then thought better about it. It was a valid question.

"I don't know yet," she said. "I have to figure it out."

They walked back through the snow and went back inside the house.

"I'll get the gun," Declan said, dashing upstairs.

It was bad when a nine-year-old knew where the guns were.

And even worse that he knew how to shoot. They'd both spent some time outside practicing. But that was so they could hunt for food. At least that's what she told him.

Something was nagging at the back of her mind.

Something other than the knowledge that they couldn't just shoot the man. Maybe he was just passing through. Maybe heading home.

And needed someplace warm to rest. Someplace out of the snow.

A minute later, Declan came running back down the stairs with the gun.

"Declan, don't run with the gun."

"Sorry," he said, slowing down a little bit.

She took the gun from him. "We aren't going to shoot him."

"Because he's a southerner?"

"Because it's wrong to go around shooting people," she said.

Even Declan could tell the man was a southerner.

Declan looked up at her with big round eyes. "Natalie?"

"What is it?" she asked.

They were standing just inside the front door. What used to be a grand foyer with paintings and a grandfather clock.

But now was just an entranceway. The paintings and clock had been taken by the Yankees. What was left, she and Declan had used for firewood.

"I'm hungry," Declan said.

They had no food here in the main house. The only way to get something for them to eat was to go into the kitchen.

"Dang it," Natalie leaned against the wall. There was no easy answer.

"Dang it," Declan echoed.

Natalie covered her face to hide a smile.

It was times like this that reminded her that he was still just a child.

It was so easy to forget.

Natalie was seventeen. Eight years older than Declan. She should be thinking about getting married about now.

Not contemplating whether or not they were going to have to shoot a man who'd camped out in their kitchen.

Shoot a man or starve.

Surely there was another option.

They'd even stopped keeping firewood in the house.

So if they didn't get to the kitchen, they would not only starve to death, they'd freeze to death.

She had to do something.

There had to be another answer.

"You stay here," she said. "I'll go ask him to leave."

She checked the gun. To make sure it was loaded, even though she knew it was.

"No," Declan said. "You can't go without me." He was the grown up Declan now.

"You hang back then," she said. "Did you bring the pistol?"

"I'll go get it," he said, then darted back up the stairs to get the pistol.

Natalie stood tall and steeled herself. She had to do it. She had to confront the man. Ask him to leave. He could sleep in the stables if he needed a place to stay.

Declan made it back with the other gun and they set off again. Into the cold, blinding snow.

"Remember," Natalie said. "You hang back in case I need help. We have to believe he's a peaceful man until we learn otherwise."

Declan grinned through chattering teeth. "Innocent until proven guilty," he said.

"Exactly."

Declan stopped at the edge of the kitchen building.

Natalie straightened her shoulders and moved forward.

She could do this.

If not for herself, for Declan.

She lifted up the rifle and put her hand on the doorknob.

Just get this over with.

She opened the door slowly.

The man turned and looked at her.

He had a heavy beard. And like she'd noticed before, his clothes and demeanor were tattered. Tired.

She held the gun up, pointing it at his chest. The gun was heavy. And she knew she couldn't hold it like this very long.

She had to be quick.

"Sir," she said. "I must ask you to leave my home." She shifted her hold on the gun. "You're welcome to stay in our barn if you need a place to weather the storm."

The man straightened, but didn't stand. Looked right at her and squinted.

"Natalie," he said. He spoke her name softly. Almost reverently. Not a question. Not surprised.

Recognition skittered along Natalie's spine.

She knew this man.

He was her father.

Finding Natalie

CHAPTER 2

It had been the spring of 1861 when Papa put on his new gray uniform, mounted his dapple gray, and rode off to war.

He hadn't wanted to go. He hadn't believed in it.

Didn't want anything to do with seceding from the country. Wanted nothing to do with slavery or state's rights. His family had never owned slaves. They'd owned some indentured servants back in the day, but they'd worked their way to freedom and stayed on.

They and their children were like part of the family now, but they had their own cabins and worked their own little plot of land.

Nonetheless, Papa saw it as his duty to protect what was his. Whether that be his family, his land, or his country.

His country became the Confederacy when Tennessee seceded. So he rode off to do his part. Papa was no slacker.

They hadn't heard from him since the day he rode off. Not a single word.

How Mama kept going for so long, Natalie would never know.

But she did. She kept the faith.

She said Papa would be back. She said it every day until the day she died.

Natalie had given up long ago on Papa ever coming back.

She dreamed about him sometimes, but if she tried on purpose to remember what he looked like, she couldn't do it.

She and Declan never talked about him.

They had too much to worry about just surviving.

But Papa was sitting right here in her kitchen.

Though she didn't recognize him, she knew on a visceral level that it was her father.

She slowly lowered the rifle, standing it on the floor beside her.

"How are you, Kitten?" he asked.

Kitten. His pet name for her. She was about to dash forward. To put her arms around him.

Then she heard a movement behind her.

She turned just as Declan stepped through the door, the pistol pointed right at Papa.

"No!" she said, lunging in front of her brother, grabbing his wrist.

The sound of the gunshot deafened her.

And the pain that wracked through her body was worse than any pain she ever imagined.

She felt herself falling. Reaching for something to grab hold of. To stop her from falling. But there was nothing but air to grab hold of.

She felt her cheek scrape against the floor and everything went dark.

Finding Natalie

PREVIEW

CHAPTER 3

Natalie woke to the sound of crying.

She opened her eyes to see Declan's head down next to hers. He was sobbing.

She was in her own bed. But... it was daylight.

And there was a fire in her bedroom fireplace.

She went to put a hand on Declan's head, but it took an inordinate amount of effort to lift her hand from the bed a mere inch. So much so that she gave up and let her hand fall helplessly back against the bed.

Declan must have felt the small effort though, because he lifted his head and looked at her.

"What's wrong, Declan?" she asked. "Did you have another nightmare?"

Her mouth was so dry, she could barely get her tongue to work.

Declan wiped his eyes with his sleeve and, climbing into the bed next to her, wrapped his arms around her.

"Hey," she said. "What's wrong?"

She could move her left arm, so she soothed the back of his head with her left hand.

Declan said something, but she couldn't hear him because his face was buried against her side.

"I can't understand you," she said.

He turned his head so he could look up at her.

"Are you gonna die like Mama?" His eyes were red and his face damp from tears.

"Why?" she asked. "Why would I?"

"I shot you," he said.

Images came sliding back into place.

The cold snowfall.

The man in their kitchen.

Papa.

But nothing was making sense.

"Declan," she said, her mouth dry.

Now she knew why she couldn't move her hand. She shrugged her shoulder a bit and pain shot through her.

Declan sat back and looked at her through tear glazed eyes.

"Papa's home," he said. "And you saved his life."

She squeezed her eyes tightly shut. "I don't know what you mean."

"I didn't know who he was. So I shot him. But you took the bullet," Declan said, his eyes wide.

"How did I get here?" she asked. "In the bed."

"Doc brought you up here," Declan said, his face animated now as he warmed to the tale. "After he took out the bullet, he made a fire."

Doc was an older man. Older than Papa. Natalie couldn't picture him picking her up, much less bringing her upstairs.

Natalie wasn't very big, but Doc was kinda frail.

"Where are they now?" she asked.

"Downstairs," Declan said. Then as though it just occurred to him, he climbed down off the bed and headed toward the door. "I'll go tell them you're alive."

"Please don't," she said. But it was too late. He was already dashing out the door.

She closed her eyes. She'd just take a little nap until Declan got back.

Finding Natalie

PREVIEW

CHAPTER 4

When Natalie woke again, it was dark.

It took her a minute, but this time she knew where she was.

She was in her own bed in her own room.

The fire in the fireplace was still burning brightly, keeping the room warm.

She couldn't tell for sure if it was still snowing outside, but if she had to guess, she'd say it was. There was still that quietness that only came with snowfall. During or after.

Her papa was home from the war. She'd never expected to see him again.

Declan had been a child when Papa had left. And he'd seen so much since then. Lost so much.

He was only trying to protect his sister from a man he saw as a stranger.

But Natalie had stopped him from shooting their father.

And taken a bullet.

"How do you feel?" a man asked from the chair next to her bed.

A man with a voice as smooth as thick molasses on a warm summer day.

She swallowed. "Thirsty."

She tried to sit up, but any movement caused a shooting pain in her shoulder.

"Let me help you up," the man said. "May I?"

"Of course," she said. "Thank you."

The man adjusted the pillows behind her and helped her sit up. Then he poured a glass a water and held it while she drank.

"You're very kind... Mr?"

"I'm Doctor Alexander Avery," he said.

"Doctor?"

"Yes," he said, taking the glass and setting it on her nightstand.

"Are you the one who carried me up here?"

He laughed softly. "Yes. I hope you don't mind. Your father and I agreed that you'd be more comfortable here in your own room."

"You're not the regular doctor," she said. His voice was different. His accent didn't have the softness of a southern man.

He sat back in the chair, stretched his long legs out, and clasped his hands in his lap.

"I'm a friend of your father's," he said. "We got to know each other quite well during the war."

She closed her eyes, feeling an unexpected anger at her father. He'd left them there to fend for themselves. And hadn't even bothered to write them a letter.

Doctor Avery might have been not only a doctor but a mind reader.

"Your father wrote to you," he said. "but I doubt you got any of the letters."

She watched him out of the corner of her eyes.

"Why do you say that?" she asked. "Why wouldn't we get his letters if he wrote them?"

"Your father and I were taken prisoner shortly after our first battle," he said. "Sometimes the enemy soldiers would take the letters, but I doubt they bothered to post any of them."

"You were in prison this whole time?" she asked. The thought of her father sitting in a prison for months, even years, diffused some of her anger.

"Unfortunately, yes." He looked away, toward the fire, no doubt battling his own demons.

"That's awful," she said. "Where is he now?"

"He's with Declan."

She nodded. "Declan doesn't remember him."

"The war should have ended a long time ago." There was a sadness in his voice.

She wanted to see this man, this doctor, who had come home with her father.

But the only light was a pale glow from the fireplace.

Natalie closed her eyes again. She was so tired. So sleepy...

Keep Reading Finding Natalie...

Kathryn Kaleigh writes sweet contemporary romance, time travel romance, and historical romance.

kathrynkaleigh.com